Sophia,
Never stop
creating!
DML

by David Mark Lopez

To Holly, for my freedom

Black Marker Episode

3

Run Like a Fugitive

Maddie's Magic Markers

by David Mark Lopez

1

Maddie's Magic Markers Series
Black Marker (Three)
Run Like a Fugitve
Copyright 2005 by David Mark Lopez

ISBN# 0-9744097-2-3
ISBN# 978-0-9744097-2-6
Library of Congress Control Number: 2005905195

Published by David Mark Lopez
Bonita Springs, FL

Story and Illustrations by David Mark Lopez
Cover Illustration / Book Design by Jeff Thompson
Printed in the United States of America

What Kids, Parents and Teachers Are Saying About Maddie's Magic Markers!

I just finished reading, "Walk Like an Egyptian". It was great. Way better than Magic Treehouse. I think Mary Pope Osborne has met her match. I give it two thumbs up and five stars.

- Lauren Elizabeth, age 10

I absolutely LOVE your books!

- David, 5th grade

What an amazing day!!! The kids are still stopping by the media center and thanking me for your visit. They LOVE your books and really enjoyed your presentation.

- Barbara Chasnov, Media Specialist, Lockhart Middle School

I have thoroughly enjoyed the books. The plots of both books were full of exciting conflicts.

- Katlyn - age 11

I can't believe I had never heard of your books before. I can't wait to read the rest of them. You are the best author I've ever read.

- Kenneth, 4th grade

Your visit was truly an inspiration to creativity for our students.

- Gloria Arnold, 5th grade teacher

Black Marker Episode 3 Run Like a Fugitive

Maddie's Magic Markers

by David Mark Lopez

Table of Contents

Table of Contents
(Continued)

Chapter 1
Crackerjack

The footlights are lit. I spin slowly into the spotlight. I'm wearing the most amazing pink tutu in the history of the ballet. As I leap and pirouette, twirling around the stage, the crowd "oohs" and "aahs" with delight. My tights are a little too tight and I've got a little bit of a wedgie going, but that's o.k. This is totally fantastic and without a doubt the greatest night of my life. There's my dad on the stage videotaping my every move.

Hey, wait a minute. Stop. What's my dad doing on the stage? And why is he laughing at me? Oh my goodness, now he's standing over me. Poof!

Probably the last thing you ever want to see when you wake up in the morning is my dad standing over you with a video camera. This is definitely not funny. I pull the sheets over my head.

"What's up, Maddie? How about a big, goofy grin for the camera?"

I'm not answering because that will only encourage him.

"Maddie. Maddie. Maddie. Maggie?"
"Thanks for ruining a really great dream, Dad."
"What was it this time? Egypt again? Joan of Arc? The invention of toilet paper?"
"Not funny. Dad, did you know you have a giant booger attacking your face?"
"Wake up. It's time to go."
"Where?"

"It's time. Oh yes, it's definitely time."

"For...?"

"The power and the glory and the passion that is..., drum roll, please... baseball!"

"Kill me now."

"Move out."

"Is it Father's Day? Is it your birthday? Did I wake up in a parallel universe where baseball is something even mildly interesting?"

Let me explain a couple of things. First, my name is Maddie, NOT Maggie. This was only funny the first fifty times my dad said it, not the following four thousand times. Second, my dad has a lot of mental problems, but one of his biggest is baseball. Baseball cards, baseball music, baseball jerseys, baseball caps, baseball memorabilia, baseball on t.v., baseball on the radio, baseball on the internet, baseball movies and baseball games. Raise your hand here. Is it just me or am I the only ten year-old girl who has to watch "Field of Dreams" every January, because my dad cannot wait for Spring Training? I see that hand.

One February my dad came to visit me in Atlanta and he dragged me to Fanfest at Turner Field and he's NOT EVEN A BRAVES FAN. Sitting in the dugout in thirty-five degree weather is so much fun. Not. Then we have to go out and run the bases. The next thing I knew we're being escorted out of the stadium by a security guard.

"Hey Dad. I'm pretty sure they told us sliding into home plate was NOT PERMITTED."

"I told you I was Sid Bream and you were Francisco Cabrera."

"Huh?"

Dad started mumbling something mind-numbing about September, 1992, but all I wanted to do was get out of there. Nice job, Dad. Way to go.

Anyway, some more background information. I live with my mom in Atlanta and with my dad part of the time in Florida, but mostly on weekends. For my birthday a few months back he gave me some incredible, magic markers that have taken me back in time on a couple of amazing adventures. You should see them - they have glowing, floating liquid inside with little doohickies of silver and gold floating inside. Lately though, I have not been able to get the stupid stubborn caps off, so I haven't been anywhere for the past few months. Whenever I ask him about them he just looks at me like I just escaped from an insane asylum. He took me by the antique store where he bought them, but of course it was closed.

"O.K., Pops. Devil Rays or Marlins?" Since we live in Florida we can see either team.
"Rays."
"Dad, the Rays are the worst team in baseball history."
"Not true. 1962 New York Mets, 2003 Detroit Tigers."

If you want to waste twenty minutes of your life, just ask my dad a question about baseball. He is typically full of useless information, but he particularly knows a lot of meaningless trivia about baseball. His friend, Sean, is even worse. Whenever they get together they take turns naming dead baseball players. Der. I decided to drop it.

There were, however, a couple of good things about going to see the Devil Rays. First, they have Dippin' Dots® - "the ice cream of the future." Yummy. Next, the Rays play inside a domed stadium called Tropicana Field. If you are really lucky, there will be a couple of birds flying around during the game. I'm not kidding. So whenever my Dad or I see one of those birds we stand up and point and yell, "Bird!" This is not funny to anyone else, but it always cracks us up. One time my wicked stepmonster, Holly, got so irritated with us for doing this she swore she would never go to another game with us.

"Okey dokey, Dad. I'll go with you if I get to pick the ` music and I get some Dippin' Dots." Dad has absolutely the worst taste in music.
"No, and maybe."

We pile into the car and of course he picks something really, really terrible.

"No, Dad, please. I'm begging you. Not Ray Charles."
"What? You've got to be kidding. Ray Charles is the best. Case closed."
"How about something from this century?"
"He could do it all. Jazz, Blues, R&B, Rock, Soul, Country - you name it and he had a hit singing it. He was born in Georgia, grew up in Florida, blind by age six and orphaned at age fifteen, so he gets extra credit for all that. Plus, you're forgetting the coolest thing of all."
"Well?"
"The sunglasses."
"I surrender."

It wouldn't be so bad, but Dad plays the same song over and over and over - "You Don't Know Me." Hey Ray, I've got a news flash for you: The reason she doesn't know you love her soooooooo much is that you never tell her! We finally move on to "Hit the Road, Jack", and I fall asleep.

Eventually we get to the Trop, find our seats and settle in

for the game. Of course, we have to park five miles away because Dad is always too cheap to pay to park, so I'm sweating like a pig by the time we sit down. The good news is that the Trop is air-conditioned. Not a single bird in sight.

"Hey, Dad, how about some Dippin' Dots®?"
"Maybe."

We're a little early, so whenever they flash up a trivia question on the scoreboard, Dad yells out the answer like some kind of lunatic.

"Dad, you're annoying everyone."
"I am sooooo sorry."
"Alright, if you're such a genius tell me why they have that big baseball on the right field wall with a number forty-two right in the middle."
"Too easy."
"I'm waiting. Waiting. Waiting. Waiting."
"That's Jackie Robinson's number."
"Robinson Crusoe?"
"No, Jackie Robinson, Brooklyn Dodgers."
"Why is his number up there?"
"In 1997 Major League Baseball retired his number. No one in the major leagues can wear that number for any team."
"Because...?"
"He broke the color barrier in baseball."
"Red?"
"No."
"Blue, green, pink?"
"No, black. Before Jackie Robinson, African-Americans were not allowed to play baseball in the major leagues."

I just sat there for a minute. Since my dad was always

making stuff up to irritate me, I was trying to figure out if this was really true.

"You're kidding me, right?"
"Unfortunately, not."
"Why?"
"I never kid you."
"No, I mean about the color barrier thing."
"Fear. Ignorance. Racism."
"Like when you judge someone for the color of their skin instead of getting to know them to see what they are really like."
"Exactly."

More silence. It was hard for me to believe that at one time African Americans could not play baseball. Even I knew that Hank Aaron holds just about every single record for my favorite team, the Braves.

"I bet it was hard for him."
"You'd win. When he signed on with the Dodgers, he had to agree he wouldn't fight back."
"Really?"
"When he died Jesse Jackson said he had been immunized by God from catching the diseases he fought. He said that as a figure in history Jackie was a rock in the water creating concentric circles and ripples of new possibility."
"For other baseball players?"
"For everyone."

I thought about this for awhile and then it was almost time for the game to start. I saw all the Black and Hispanic players warming up and tried to imagine Baseball without them. Impossible. Dad had another brilliant idea that he was going to try and teach me how to keep "score". Hey, Pops, I'm pretty sure they already keep the score ON THE SCOREBOARD! Turns out he was talking about something else and I had to reluctantly admit it was kind of cool. You see, when you keep score at a baseball game you are actually keeping track of every single event that happens on the field with a secret code. It later dawned on me that this was just another way for obsessive compulsive baseball dorks (like my dad) to "enjoy" the game, but it was fun for awhile.

Here's how it works. Each player on the field is assigned a number. For instance, the pitcher is 1, the catcher is 2, the first baseman is 3 and so on. When the batter hits the ball you write down what happens using those numbers like this: if the batter grounds out to the second baseman you write in the little box by the batter's name 4-3. That means the second baseman threw the ball to the first baseman for the out. Following me? If the batter flies out to the center fielder you write F-8. F standing for "fly out". If the batter reaches first base you track the progress of the player drawing a little diamond and moving him around the bases as he advances. You can also keep track of balls and strikes, stolen bases, walks, and just about every thing else that happens in a baseball game except the birds flying over your head ("BIRD!") and the number of times you ask for Dippin' Dots® until your dad finally caves in and gets you some.

It took me awhile to catch on and figure it all out, but by the third inning I had a pretty good idea of how to keep "score" at a baseball game. Dad even turned loose of the scorecard and let me fill in the little squares while he went to get the Dippin' Dots®. The game was moving right along and before I knew it we were in the seventh inning. Turned out that keeping "score" made the whole game a lot more interesting in my ten year-old opinion.

"Dad, it's almost time for the seventh-inning stretch."

Silence.

"Hey, Dad. You must not have heard me a few seconds ago. I said, 'It's almost time for the seventh-inning stretch.'"
"And..."
"That means more ICE CREAM OF THE FUTURE."
"Do you have a tapeworm?"
"Come on, Dad. I've been pretty good today, listening to Ray Charles, pretending to be interested in the Rays, learning to keep score - what about it?"
"I'll take it under consideration."
"We also have another major problem."
"What now?"
"Broken pencil."

The first half of the inning ended and to my shock and surprise Dad jumped up and started up the aisle hopefully not just to go to the bathroom.

"Dad?"

He turned and looked at me as he was heading up the steps.

"Don't forget the pencil."
"Here, catch." He pulled a pen out of his pocket and tossed it to me. It was a little over my head, but I reached up and snagged it.
"F-8."
"Huh?"
"You'd make a pretty good center fielder."

He turned and trotted out of sight.

After we all sang "Take Me Out to the Ballgame", (I always sing, "buy me some peanuts and Dippin' Dots®") the bottom half of the inning started with no sign of my dad, so I pulled off the pen cap and started tracking the balls and strikes of the first hitter. The Rays were trying to get a rally going so the organ player cranked up the "Mexican Hat Dance" music. You know, Dun-dun-de-dun-dun-de-dun-DUN-DUN, (clap, clap). I couldn't resist humming along.

You know, when weird things happen to you, they never happen in order like in a book or a movie. They happen to you suddenly, all at once, and you have to try and remember later what really happened. I was totally focused on the score card, so it kind of surprised me when I smelled a familiar odor coming from the pen. I glanced at the pen and it slowly dawned on me the pen in my hand, the one my dad had casually lobbed to me a few minutes ago, the one that the aroma was coming from, was the BLACK MAGIC MARKER from my actual magic magical marker set. The cap was off, the magic marker was glowing, the music was playing and...then I noticed everyone around me was standing up and yelling their fool heads off.

I glanced over just in time to see my Dad out of the corner of my eye coming down the steps, pointing up with one hand, holding the Dippin' Dots® in the other and trying to tell me something. Bird? I then looked up just in time to see a foul ball, like a giant meteorite getting bigger by the second, crash land on my forehead. Bonk.

The last thing I think I saw was my dad swinging an imaginary baseball bat. Fade... to... black.

"THE TROP"

Chapter 2
RatFink

I don't get headaches very often, but this one was a doozy. It felt like someone was poking a screwdriver into my eye. I reached up and gently touched the gigantic bump on my forehead. Yowwwwwwweeeee. I discovered that my eye was swollen shut about halfway and something truly disgusting was oozing out of that lump I just touched. I was probably going to have a shiner for the next two weeks. On top of that my good eye was watering and I couldn't see a thing. Other than those problems, everything was just terrific.

Drip. Drip. Drip. As my mind started to clear I realized that one of the reasons I couldn't see very well is that it was mostly dark. Drip. Drip. Drip. The last thing I remembered was the baseball doinking me on the head. I squinted my eyes (ouch), shook my head (big mistake) and tried to gather my thoughts. Drip. Drip. Drip. What was that noise? It had to be the sound of water dripping. At least I hoped it was water.

I gradually realized that I probably wasn't at the "Trop" anymore and that I had once again landed somewhere in history. That's when I noticed the smell. Don't worry; I've smelled plenty of bad things before: my dad's cooking, Thing Two's (my little brother) disgusting dirty diapers and the boys in my class after P.E., but I guarantee you I'd never smelled anything that even came close to this. It smelled like a combination of low tide, an overripe diaper and a dumpster full of rotting food. It was all I could do to keep from vomiting. Yuck.

1 I was standing up and leaning against a
irface that was both wet and slimy. Lovely.
iinst the wall and moved my feet along the
I was standing on. To my horror it only
's in each direction before it dropped off
ᵕ wnat. Drip. Drip. Drip. I took my hands off
ᵕᵤ, wiped them on my pants and tried to figure out what
to do next. The one thing I'd learned from my other trips was
not to panic.

After I stood there for a few minutes hearing the water drip
and smelling that awful smell my eyesight began to adjust to
the darkness. I could tell that I wasn't in a cave, because I
could make out a faint circle of light in the distance and some
of the objects around me started to take shape. That dripping
water had to be coming from somewhere above me.
Hmmmm.

The smell. The water. Round walls. Faint light in the
distance. Then it hit me just like that baseball smacking me
right between the eyes. I was in an UNDERGROUND
SEWER. Wonderful. Nice job, black marker. I guess it
would have been too much trouble just landing me in a feather
bed somewhere or maybe a candy factory. Almost anything
would have been better than this.

O.K. This wasn't the end of the world. If I was right and
this was a sewer, then somewhere above me was a city. A city
full of people. People who could tell me when and where I
was. The trick was going to be getting out of this stinky mess
and up into that city. Time to swing into action. I decided my
best bet was to head toward that dim circle of light in the
distance.

Step one was to get off of the ledge I was standing on. I

squatted down and stuck my leg over as far as I could. I felt the wall curving inward slightly the further I reached. This would be a lot easier if my head wasn't pounding like a freight train. No matter how far I reached I still was only touching the wall. I thought I heard something besides the water dripping, so I yelled a couple of times just in case there was someone close enough to hear me. Nothing. The only thing that accomplished was making my head hurt worse.

My only choice was to get off that ledge and move toward the light. I got down on my knees and slowly began lowering myself over the edge. My fingers gripped the damp ledge and my knees scraped along the curved edge of the wall. I still wasn't hitting anything except the wall and my fingers began to slowly slip from the ledge. Not good. I finally gave up and let go and dropped another couple of feet scraping my knees as I went. I landed with a plop into some wet, gooey, slimy water about half way up to my knees. Completely and totally disgusting. Now I knew where the smell was coming from. I tried not to think about what I was standing in.

It wasn't going to do me any good to stand there and try not to barf. I pulled one foot out of the sticky slop and then the other and started heading toward the dim light ahead of me. Because of my half-swollen eye and the almost total darkness I had no way of knowing how far away the light was or how long it would take. My Dippin' Dots day was turning into a complete disaster.

Every once in awhile as I was struggling through the muck, I would run into something solid like a piece of wood or a big clump of garbage. Since I couldn't see anything ahead of me this made me lose my balance and I had to put my hand down into the mess to keep from falling. It wasn't long before I was pretty much covered from head to toe with this foul smelling slime.

The only good news is that I was slowly but surely getting closer to the light ahead of me. I just kept moving forward the best I could and hoped that there was a hot shower somewhere in my near future. I started to notice that the sludge I was wading through was getting a little deeper every few feet or so. I hadn't really been paying attention, so I wasn't actually sure whether this was true or not. I made an effort to keep track of how far up my leg the goo was sloshing. Every once in awhile I thought I heard some noises, but whenever I stopped to listen the noise stopped too. Creepy.

The closer I got to the light the more I could make out my surroundings. I was definitely wading in a river of garbage in a gigantic round pipe of some sort. Ahead of me the light was streaming down from above. It looked like there was some kind of ladder curving around the wall up to the place where the light was coming through. All right! All I had to do was climb up the ladder and crawl out. I couldn't wait to get out of this stinking, slimy mess.

Finally, I was getting somewhere. I struggled the last few yards to the ladder, but it was very clear the yuck I was wading through was getting deeper. When I got to the ladder it didn't take me long to figure out that it was rusty and slippery from all the underground moisture. Out of the corner of my eye I thought I saw something moving, but I was too preoccupied with the ladder to notice. I took one step up to the first rung and almost lost my shoe in the scudge. The first few rungs were easy enough, but I was going to have some trouble getting all the way up. Since the ladder curved, I had to pull myself up by hand, rung by rung, until my feet were dangling beneath me. It was like an uphill monkey bar, but I was determined to get to the top.

That's when disaster struck. When I finally got to the top I could see through what must have been a manhole cover to the outside. I was really getting tired, but I managed to haul myself up by my elbow onto the last rung and push the iron cover with my free hand. It didn't budge. I pushed and pushed as hard as I could, but it just wouldn't move. Then I pushed so hard, I started slipping and after a few desperate seconds I plopped about ten feet down into the river of garbage, mud and who knows what else. The only good news is that it broke my fall, but I still ended up sitting waist deep in the world's smelliest slime. Did I mention that I had a headache?

I yelled a few times hoping someone outside could hear me. I yelled and yelled as loud as I could, but no one came. Let me rephrase that. No person came. At the edge of the sewer, where the liquid met the wall sat a fat, hairy, black rat.

My knowledge of sewers and rats was somewhat limited, since I was used to living ABOVE GROUND. My only experience with sewers came from - you guessed it - Dad.

"Yo, Dad."
"Yup."
"Where're we going?"
"Who wants to know?"
"Your mama."
"Very, very impolite."
"Just tell me."
"We are going to the theatre for your information, madame."
"Must we?"

"We must."

"What movie are we going to see?"

"Who said anything about a movie?"

"You did."

"Did not."

"Did so."

"Not."

"So."

"I said,"We are going to the theatre."

So to make a long story short and eliminating a lot of confusing chatter from Pops, he took me to see 'Les Miserables' when I was just a kid. Have you ever seen that musical? I didn't think I would like it, but I ended up loving it and learning all the songs and singing them over and over and over until my dad finally told me to "shut up" or he was never taking me anywhere again. O.K. here's the point. In Les Mis, Jean Valjean had to carry young Marius underground through the sewers of Paris to save him. He got out and so could I. However, I don't remember anything about rats.

I looked at the rat. He looked at me. What did I know about rats? Almost nothing. Rats carry disease. They can bite you. They hang around garbage. They are not nice - like the mice, for instance, you might find in Cinderella. In all this smelly garbage, there was probably more than just this one rat who was staring me down. Then I found out something about rats I didn't know. The rat jumped (I'm not making this up) into the river of garbage and started swimming through the ooze toward me.

After I got over the shock and surprise of seeing the rat swimming, I got moving. I got off my rear end and headed back toward the ladder. I pulled myself up again and held on while the rat climbed back out of the ick about five feet away.

The light was a little better beneath the manhole and my one good eye was finally adjusting to the dimness. That's when I noticed, to my horror, all the other rats.

They were everywhere. Dozens of them. I could not believe I hadn't noticed them before. Maybe I woke them up with all my yelling. They were on both sides of "scum river" and they all seemed to be looking at me. One of the rats was bigger and longer than all the others. He was about the size of a football and seemed to be feared by all the other rats. Whenever he moved the other rats stayed out of his way. King Rat. He was slowly and steadily moving toward my perch on the ladder. My hands were slippery from the slime and I was losing my grip. My day was about to get much worse.

I looked both ways down the tunnel and discovered that there was another dim light further down in the opposite direction. I must not have noticed it before. I could either waste all my energy hanging onto this ladder with the rats waiting for me to drop in for dinner or head in that direction. I reluctantly climbed up two more rungs, hung down by my arms and released into the mire. I landed with a plop and before I started striding forward I saw at least three rats jump into the "water" behind me. King Rat started running along the wall beside me with all the other rats close behind. They were having fun. I was not.

What's worse than being chased? Being chased in the dark by rats in a river of sludge, that's what. I started plowing ahead but the going was getting tougher because the filth was up to my waist. I hoped the swimming rats were having as hard a time as I was. I turned and looked back. It was getting darker as I moved away from the ladder, but the rats were definitely gaining on me. Time for full-blown PANIC mode.

I literally started leaping and sloshing through the stinking muck. This actually made things worse, because every few feet I would stumble and fall face first into the goo. When the first rat reached me I almost had a heart attack. He latched onto my arm and I flung him all the way to the wall. I turned and picked up something out of the garbage and faced the army of swimming rats coming toward me. I started swinging like crazy hoping to keep them at bay. I knew this wasn't going to work for long, but I was getting desperate. King Rat was at the edge of the gunk leading his troops to the battle. I whacked every rat that came close, but there were too many for me to hold out. Desperate times call for desperate measures.

I dropped whatever I was holding, turned toward the light, held my breath and dove into the scum creek and started swimming as hard as I could. I could feel the rats swimming beside me trying to climb onto my back and legs. I surfaced. The good news - the light was getting closer. The bad news - a rat was on my head. I grabbed him by the tail, threw him and dove back into the goop. When the rats started biting my legs and arms, I swam with all my might. By the time I finally reached the light and the ladder (thank goodness for that ladder) the water was teeming with rats and I was over my head in scum. I grabbed for the lowest rung and pulled myself up, shaking the rats off me.

When I finally got up out of the sludge, I held onto the ladder, and kicked the last rat off my leg. I realized I was completely and totally exhausted. My eye was still swollen shut, my head was still pounding and now I was covered with dozens of stinging rat bites and the smelliest slime you could ever imagine. I slowly wiped my good eye and looked up. Finally some wonderful news - the manhole cover above me was half open and if I could just drag myself up I a few more rungs I would be free. Free at last. Free at last.

Even better, there was a tiny ledge on the wall of the pipe where I could stop and rest for a few minutes. I stepped over and watched the rats swimming in their crazed frenzy. I waited a few minutes and started the agonizing climb back up the slippery ladder. Then I saw the worst thing I had seen in this miserable, smelly stinkhole. Two rungs up the ladder, between me and freedom sat the one and only, his eminence, King Rat. How in the world did he get up there? I looked into his beady, red eyes and watched as his whiskers twitched in the dim light. He bared his teeth and dared me to come up.

I stepped back onto the narrow ledge and fell to my knees. The tears welled up in my eyes and every square inch of my body was spent. I wanted to scream and cry at the same time. Then something happened to me that has never happened before. A slow-burning rage quietly filled my soul and then spread quickly through my body like an electric shock. I had had just about enough of these ridiculous rats and their smelly sewer. No way was I going to let King Rat and his nasty pals beat me. I reached down into the stinking, fetid scudge one last time and pulled out a board about the size of a baseball bat.

I slowly stood up on the ledge and looked into the sneering face of King Rat. I gathered my last remaining ounce of energy, swung from my heels and jacked that fat monster deep into the cheap seats in the centerfield bleachers. GOING…GOING…GONE! It's outta here!!!!

Scorecard reads: HR/8. Maddie 1, Rats 0.

I dropped the board and climbed the last few rungs to my freedom.

Chapter 3
Mission Impossible

I was so tired when I dragged my weary bones into the sunlight; I could barely hold my head up. It took me a couple of seconds for my eyes to make the adjustment from almost total darkness to daylight. When the horse almost stepped on my head, it definitely got my attention.

"Hey, pal, watch where you're going!"

Then I saw a wagon getting ready to roll right over the top of me. I ducked back down into the hole as it rumbled over me. I stuck my head out one more time and took in the scene around me. I couldn't make out much of anything, except a bunch of burned out buildings and a lot of horse and foot traffic. At that very second a newspaper blew across my face completely blocking my view. I grabbed the newspaper and read the gigantic headline screaming across the top of the page, "LEE SURRENDERS AT APPOMATTOX". My head started spinning. Richmond Register April 10th, 1865. 1865? 1865!

I sat there, stunned. April 10th, 1865. The Civil War was almost over. I wasn't such a great history student, but I looked at my fingers and started counting. One, two, three, four. Another horse almost stepped on me, but I barely noticed it. Thanks to my "crazy about the Civil War" teacher, Mrs. Pinkston, every snot-nosed kid in my fourth grade class knew what had happened on April 14th, 1865. I got a sick feeling in the pit of my stomach. In four days President Abraham Lincoln was going to be MURDERED! Shot in the head by a cold-blooded killer.

Despite my terrible physical condition I went numb. I slumped over in the dirty street, half in and half out of the hole. The roar of history was filling my ears and my head. Civil War...Lincoln...Assassination...Richmond. Actually maybe that wasn't the roar of history, it was that team of horses and a carriage coming straight at me. I couldn't move. Just as a gigantic hoof almost smashed my face, someone grabbed me by the collar and dragged me to safety.

I looked up at the person dragging me, but because of the sunlight and my bad eye I couldn't make him out. He stopped dragging me when we got to the boardwalk. My eyes focused and I discovered it was another kid just like me, only a lot skinnier and a lot taller. He looked like a broomstick with teeth. Before I could say a word he bent over and stuck his freckled-face and flaming red haired head right into my face.

"Watcha doin' in my hole, girlie-girl? Tryin to get runned over?"

"What do you mean, your hole?"

'Everbody knows 'round here that I'm the rat catcher and them there holes in the street are my bidness."

"You're the rat catcher?"

"That's the fact, ma'am."

"Oh, really."

"Darn- tootin."

"I've got a news flash for you then."

"How's that?"

"You missed a couple of thousand rats down in the sewer, Bud, and they just about had me for lunch!"

"Shudna been down there in the first place."

"No kidding."

I just sat there for a minute with this goofy looking kid staring at me.

"You look like you've been rode hard and put away wet, Stinky."
"Thanks. It's my new perfume. It's called 'eau de sewage'."
"Ain't seen you round here before. Got a name, missy?"
"Are you writing a book?"
"Caint read nor write fo' yo information."
"My name is Maddie. How about you? You got a name or are you just called 'Ratboy'?"
"Names Jebediah Conroy Akins."
"Big name for a skinny kid."
"I ain't no kid, Maggie. Mostly twelve years old goin' on thirteen. My friends jus call me 'Noodles'. Pleased ta meet ya."

He stuck out his skinny, freckled hand and grinned like a monkey.

I guess he was harmless enough.

"My pleasure, but the name's Maddie. Thanks for pulling me out of the way, Noodles."
"Twernt nothing, Maggie."
"MADDIE!"
"Take it easy, girlie-girl."

As I sat there taking stock of my situation, an amazing thought started to form in my brain. I suddenly realized the whole reason I had been sent on this trip back to the Civil War. This time, instead of just participating in history, I was going to have a chance to make history. Suddenly it all made sense and I forgot all about my swollen eye, the rat bites, my fatigue and that incredibly bad smell which was probably me. My job was to stop the assassination of President Lincoln. I had to get to Washington, D.C. sometime in the next four days and warn the President. Time to swing into action!

"Ok, Noodles, I need your help."
"I'm thinkin' I already did jus that."
"Of course you did, and even though I wasn't very nice to you at first, I really appreciate it."
"That's more like it. 'Noodles the ratcatcher' at your service."

He bent low with a sweep of his arm and an exaggerated bow. Then he fell over.

I tried not to laugh as he scrambled to his feet. He turned beet red.

"Um, Noodles?"
"Yup."
"Got some straw in your hair."
"Mebbe I do, but I still look and SMELL a whole lot better than you."
"You need to take me to a police station."
"A what? Pole-cat station?"
"You know, police, law and order, badges, guns, etc."
"Sounds like a sojer to me."
"That'll do. Can you help me find a soldier?"
"What kind you want, Yankee or Johnny Reb?"
"Who's in charge?"
"Did ya just fall out the turnip truck? The Confederates bout burnt this place to the ground when they left last week."

I looked around at what had to be Richmond, Virginia.

Noodles was right. The smell of smoke filled the air and just about every building I could see was either still smoldering or already burned to the ground.

"Can you find me a Union Soldier?"
"Ain't too hard. Jus look around."

Noodles turned his head and gestured behind him. He was right. There were plenty of soldiers in blue uniforms and they all seemed to be in a hurry.

I knew none of them would stop and listen to me, so I needed to talk to someone who was important enough to hear my story.

"Can you take me to someone who's in charge?"
"I think they done set up in the tabaccy warehouse over yonder. Let's try that."

Noodles started to lead the way, but as I stood up to walk all my physical problems came rushing back and I stumbled into the street."

"Whoa, Nelly. Let's get you cleaned up a mite fore we go a visitin'."

He helped me up and took me back behind some of the burned-out buildings, where he showed me an old pump. Noodles helped me wash some of the dried muck off me and gave me a rag to cleanse out my rat bites. Fortunately, none of them looked serious and if I didn't catch a disease I figured I would live.

"Now you look a little more presentable and not quite so stinky."

"Thanks."

"Why you wanna talk to them sojers anyhow?"

"I'll tell you, but you have to promise to keep it a secret."

"Shucks. I'm great at keepin' a secret."

"Swear."

"I swear." He spat in his hand, stuck it out and leaned in.

I declined the hand and whispered.

"Someone is trying to kill President Lincoln."

He stood up, threw his head back and started laughing like a donkey.

"Hee-haw. Hee-haw. Hee-haw."

"What's so funny, Ratboy?"

"Maggie, that's your big secret? That's what you want to tell the Yanks?"

"It's Maddie, and please keep your voice down!"

He was yelling now.

"Hey everybody! Maddie says someone wants to kill ole Honest Abe!"

"Ok, genius, now that everybody knows, what's so darn funny?"

"Maddie, half the people in this country want to kill President Lincoln!"

I thought about this for a minute and realized that old Noodles was probably right. I jumped up and grabbed him by the face with one hand and stared into his pale blue eyes.

"But I know where it's going to happen, when it's going to happen, how it's going to happen and who is going to do it."

This was mostly true, but I could not remember who was going to do the killing or exactly where it was.

When he saw how serious I was, he stopped laughing. He slapped my hand away and sobered up.

"Alright, alright. Let's get goin' then, but I ain't got all day. I got rats to catch."
"I think I know where maybe you can find a few."
"Better be watchin' your mouth or I'll be usin' you for bait."

I followed him down an alley and back out onto the main road. We walked a couple of blocks among the smoldering buildings and the streets teeming with Yankee soldiers.

Before long we got to headquarters and Noodles pointed me in the right direction. I climbed up the steps and found my way blocked by a couple of big guys with guns and blue uniforms.

"Excusssseeee me!"
"Sorry, can't let you pass."
"It's urgent that I speak with the officer in charge."
"Not today. We're a little busy."
"I have urgent news of the utmost importance that I have to give to the person in charge."
"Keep moving."
"You have to let me in. If you don't something terrible is going to happen."
"Like what?"
"Someone is going to kill the President."
"They should have done that last week when he was here."
"Where is he now?"

"Back in Washington."

"I'm not kidding. I know someone who is trying to kill President Lincoln."

"So do I."

"You do?"

"Everybody in this town who isn't a Negro or a Union soldier."

This wasn't going well and I was getting nowhere. I tried to push my way through and the soldier used his gun to shove me to the ground. I got up, dusted myself off, and made another charge this time yelling like a banshee. The soldier again blocked my way, but this time he dropped his gun and grabbed me by the wrists. A crowd was starting to gather.

He pulled me close. I could smell his nasty breath.

"I've had just about enough of you, Stinky Girl. You can either go quietly or I'm going to put you under arrest. It's up to you."

I poked him in the eye. He yelped and pushed me down again.

I figured if he arrested me at least I would have a chance to tell someone about what was going to happen. I gathered for another run at it, when Noodles swooped in, grabbed me by the waist and started pulling me down the street. I kicked and screamed and pounded him with my fists, but he held on tight until we got to the end of the block.

"Are you plumb out of yo head?"

"I've got to do something!"

"If they arrest you, they'll throw you in the pokey or the orphanage. I been in both of those places and I guarantee ya, you don't want to be in neither one."

Just then I heard someone yell,

"There she is! Get her!"

A group of Yankee soldiers was coming right at us with rifles and bayonets raised.

"Maggie, we'd better high-tail it or you're a goner. Follow me!"

I tried to follow Noodles down a dark, smoky alley, but one of the soldiers grabbed me. I stomped on his foot and wiggled my way out of his outstretched grasp. I ran like the wind and realized that changing history was going to be a lot harder than I thought.

Chapter 4
Funeral for a Friend

I've got to hand it to Noodles. The kid knew his way around Richmond. I followed him through alleys, open doorways, burned out buildings, switchbacks, behind houses, stores, and through the war-torn streets of downtown Richmond. He was so good at losing the soldiers following us we almost ran into the back of them several times. The best part was when he ran them through a stockyard on the edge of town. I didn't mind the pigpen since I was already covered with the stink from the sewer, but the soldiers looked a might peeved when they fell over the pigsty into the slop and mud and came out smelling like pig poop and covered with chicken feathers. At that point they finally gave up, but I saw a couple of them waving their fists at us as we ran out of sight.

We finally stopped running when we couldn't see the Yankees anymore. I followed Noodles into a clearing and we crashed behind a couple of trees. We were both gasping for air and doubled over with laughter.

"I ain't had that much fun since we let them rats go in the schoolhouse."
"I take it that happy day was the end of your formal education."
"Darn tootin'. The schoolmarm figgered if I liked rats so much, she'd put me to work."
"Lucky you."
"Twern't no good at letters anyhow."
"Well you sure know your way around Richmond."
"Much obliged."

I looked at my new friend, Noodles. He was kind of cute if you looked at him the right way. Hopefully I was not getting one of those weird crushes like I had on my cousin Daniel a few months back.

"Noodles, how far is it to Washington?"
"You joshin'me?"
"No, I'm not kidding. I've got to get to Washington, and it's pretty clear I'm not going to get any help from any soldiers anytime soon."
"Don't matter, no how."
"Why?"
"Even if ya'll knew how to get there, there's no way in heck TO get there. The bridges outta the city have all been burnt up and the road to Washington is crawlin' with Yankees, Rebs, Contrabands, thieves and free slaves. No place for a little bitty girl."
"I'm not that little."

He just stared at me. Then he scratched his head and stared at his shoes. I could tell he was thinking. Several minutes went by.

"Noodles…?"
"Yup."
"What are you thinking?"
"Too early to tell. You wait here and I'll be back in an hour or so. I might jus' know a way to get you out of here."
"Really?"
"Don't get yer hopes up. It's over a hunnert miles to Washington. Whatever happens stay right here. I'll be back."
"Noodles, I'm running out of time. Please, please, please hurry."

"At your service, ma'am."

He gave me his famous bow, this time without falling, and slipped out of sight. I closed my eyes and tried to take a little nap, but my mind wouldn't shut off.

Only four days left and half of one was already gone. I had to get to Washington somehow, find President Lincoln and warn him. It didn't take me long to realize that it wasn't going to be easy if today was any indication. I knew I would have a tough time actually getting to see the President. I might have better luck just trying to stop his killer. I put on my thinking cap and tried to remember everything I could about the assassination. I knew it happened in the evening when Honest Abe and his wife were attending the theater. What else? The name of the theatre started with an "F". I named everything I knew starting with that letter: French fries, football, five, feathers, frogs, Fred Flintstone, fort… wait a minute…was that it…Fort's Theater? That was close. I needed to remember that.

Just then I noticed how hungry I was. It had to be past lunch time and I was starving. Thinking about French fries must have set off my lunch alarm. Ding, ding, ding. I tried to go back to thinking about history, but it was no use. I knew Noodles told me to stay put, but maybe I could bum some bread or something to keep my stomach from roaring.

I edged out from behind the trees and crossed the clearing to the road.

Major mistake. Just about the exact second I stepped onto the road I was spotted by one of the "chicken-feather gang". When the soldier shouted I started running even though I had no idea where I was going. There was no point in going back to the trees since they'd find me there in about two seconds. I looked back and ran smack into Noodles coming the other way. We both hit the ground and my swollen eye screamed with new found pain.

"Maddie, what in godforsaken holy tarnation…"
"No time now, Noodles, we have got to hit the road, Jack."

I pointed to the rapidly approaching soldier. Noodles, whose nose was bleeding, shot me a look of rage, grabbed my arm, dragged me to my feet and we were off and running again. Since we were on the outskirts of town, it was much harder this time to get away. In fact, soon the soldier on the ground was joined by others on horseback. Every time we thought we lost them another one would pop up right in front of us. They finally had us cornered and I was ready to give up when Noodles saved us again.

We ducked into a saloon and sprinted up some stairs with a soldier in hot pursuit. Noodles and I burst into someone's bedroom, I gave them a little wave, and we scrambled out onto a narrow balcony. A supply wagon passed below, Noodles looked at me, grabbed my hand and we leaped together onto some flour sacks in the back of the moving wagon. We burrowed under the sacks and hoped for the best. After a couple of blocks we dug our way out and jumped onto the street. There was no sign of the soldiers, but Noodles was extremely unhappy. He glared at me and dusted the flour off his clothes. He wiped the blood and snot off his face with the back of his hand.

"Didn't I tell you to stay put, Maggie!"
"It's Maddie, and you don't have to shout."

This only made him madder and he spluttered and

stuttered.

"Here I go stickin' my neck out for you and you caint even do the one simple little thing I told you to do."
"Sorry, I got hungry."
"Them sojers got plenty of vittles. You should jus' go with them."
"Noodles, I'm sorry."
"You sure say that a lot."
"I know."

When I started brushing the flour out of my hair and off my face, he just started laughing.

"What?"
"You sure are a sight for sore eyes. I reckon you've had a pretty rough day."
"Der."
"Here you go. This'll make you feel better."

He tore me off a piece of bread from a loaf he pulled from his pocket.

"Where'd you get that?"
"I grabbed some off a table in the saloon."
"Noodles, you are simply amazing."

I shoved the bread in my mouth.

"That's what I've been tryin' to tell ya, Stinky."

After we wolfed down the bread he signaled for me to follow him. I started to ask him where we were going, but he just put his finger to his lips and ambled down the street like he was the king of the world.

We kept to the side of the road and tried to draw as little attention to ourselves as possible. We changed directions frequently and kept a sharp eye out for the soldiers who had been chasing us. There were plenty of soldiers around, but none of them seemed to recognize us, so we made pretty good time. We stopped at a pump to get some water, and I tried to get some more info from Noodles.

"So, Noodles, where are we going?"
"I may have jus' found a way to get you to Washington."
"How?"
"Moses."
"Moses?"
"Yup. If anyone can get you there, it's Moses."
"Ok, so where is he?"
"Right over there."

He pointed across the street to a stable. The only thing that I saw was a short, stocky, mysterious looking black woman.

"I don't see him."
"Lookin' right at 'em."
"Where is he?"
"Right in front of yer eyes."
"Where?"
"Come on."

He dragged me across the street and we stopped in front of the stable. The black woman looked at me with piercing eyes.

"Moses, this is Maggie, I mean Maddie. She's the one I tol' you 'bout that is needin' yer help."

I thought he was kidding. This was the Moses who was supposed to help me get through the treacherous road to

Washington? Was Noodles playing a joke on me, getting me back for all the trouble I caused him? The woman said nothing, but motioned for us to follow her into the dark stable. I wasn't too keen on following her, but I had finally learned to trust Noodles. As my eyes adjusted to the darkness I noticed two horses hitched to a loaded wagon. We stooped down as Moses whispered.

"I can help you get to Washington, but you must do exactly as I say without any questions. If you want to get out of town today, we must move quickly. I'll explain later, but we don't have any time to discuss it now."

I looked at her and gulped. This was a tough choice. I was determined to get to Washington and this was probably my only chance. I nodded my head in agreement.

She lit a lantern and quickly pulled herself onto the back of the wagon.

"Climb up."

I did as she instructed. She stood beside the long box that was loaded on the wagon. She stared at me and then looked at the long, rectangular box.

"What?"
"We've got to pretend we're taking a body to a funeral out of town. That's the only way they will let us on one of the barges to get across the river."

I took a close look at the box in the dim light. It was not just a box. It was a casket. A casket for DEAD PEOPLE.

"Who's funeral?"

Moses stood silently in front of me, lifted the lid and motioned for me to get in the box.

"Yours."

Creepy, creepy and even more creepy. My skin started to crawl. I slowly lowered myself in, she shut the box and I was once again surrounded by total darkness.

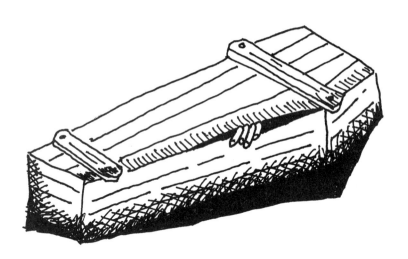

Chapter 5
Minty Fresh

I have to admit after I got over the weirdness of being in a coffin I kind of drifted off to sleep. I was pretty worn out from fighting the rats and running from the soldiers. I remember the wagon starting and stopping a couple of times and I know I heard someone say in a loud voice, "Bringin' out the dead, now." They must have been talking about me. We may have also been on water, but I'm not too sure. I finally drifted off into a deep sleep for who knows how long. The next thing I knew, someone was prying open the lid to my "bed" and there was Noodles standing over me with this big, idiotic grin on his face.

"Well, yer snorin' purdy good for a dead person."
"First of all I don't snore and I'm definitely not dead."
"Coulda fooled me."

I clambered out of the box and hopped down off the stopped wagon into the moonlight. My legs were so stiff and sore I almost fell over. Evidently night had fallen during my "funeral." I looked around. Noodles was still on the wagon and the strange, black woman who had put me in the coffin was in the driver's seat, holding the reins.

"Hey, Maddie, come 'round here. Got sommun I want ya ta meet."

Noodles hopped into the front of the wagon and I slowly walked around. I looked up into the scrunched up, very serious face of the person who had spirited me out of Richmond.

"Moses, this is Maddie."

I warily reached up to shake her hand. She just stared at me for a few seconds and then her face broke into a beautiful smile. She reached down and pulled me up into the front of the wagon.

"Name's really Harriet, but my friends call me, Minty."
"Nice to meet you, Minty."
"How'd you like your trip out of Richmond?"
"That was a little unusual, but it looks like it worked."
"Just a little trick I learned riding the rails."
"You worked on the railroads?"
"Something like that. We've got to get moving if we want to get you to Washington. I hear you are on a very important mission."

Finally an adult who didn't think I was just some crazy kid. I settled in between Minty and Noodles and the horses kept us moving at a nice rocking pace.

"So what was your job on the railroad?"
"I was a conductor."
"Really?"

Noodles started laughing.

"What's so funny, Rat-boy?"
"Maggie, Moses worked for the Underground Railroad."

I thought about that for a minute, trying to figure out if they had subways in the middle of the 1800's and/or what an underground railroad might actually look like. I thought Noodles was yanking my chain and was about to say so, when it hit me like a thunderbolt. Ka-boom. I slowly turned and looked at the tiny, black woman sitting next to me, driving the horses. I was sitting next to history. This was Harriet Tubman, the person who helped hundreds of slaves escape the South on the Underground Railroad.

"Oh my goodness. YOU ARE HARRIET TUBMAN!"
"Child, keep your voice down. Of course I am - who did you think I was?"
"I had no idea I was ..."

I stopped and wondered if Harriet really knew how famous she had become. Did she know that millions of school children studied and admired her life every year? I doubted it. I decided to keep my mouth shut.

"No idea what?"
"Uh, no idea I would have so much trouble getting out of Richmond."
"These are dangerous times."
"Thank you so much for helping me. Are you going to take me all the way to Washington?"
"I'll take you as far as I can. We can't keep this borrowed wagon much longer, but I'll help you the rest of the way on foot. I know a few folks who may be able to help us out along the way. We'll be traveling most of the way at night and try to rest some in the daytime."
"Just like on the Underground Railroad, right?"

Harriet let out a chuckle. We road along in silence for a long time. The moon was bright and there must have been a million twinkling stars throwing out their lights. It was so exciting to be on this amazing adventure. I decided to see if I could learn some more about my famous rescuer.

"Hey Harriet - I mean Minty, do you think you could tell

me about what it was like when you were a little girl?"
"What you want to know about that for?"
"Just curious, I guess."
"Nothin' but hard times."
"You were a slave, right?"

She didn't answer and we sat in silence for a few minutes.
I think Noodles had fallen asleep because he slumped over in
my direction. Finally she answered in a small, quiet voice.
Almost a whisper.

"You sure you want to hear about this?"
"Why wouldn't I?"
"It's not pretty."
"I can take it."
"I was born into slavery on a plantation on the eastern
    shore of Maryland. I was blessed because most of the
    time I got to live with my parents and my brothers and
    sisters."
"What do you mean most of the time?"
"Two of my older sisters were sold off to other slaveholders.
    I never saw them again."
"Oh."
"I don't remember much about being little. My daddy
    made me a cradle of wood and every once in awhile the
    white women from the big house would come and play
    with me. By the time I was five the master had already
    hired me out to my first job."
"Five?"
"Five."

I tried to get my mind around that. When I was five I was
in kindergarten. The only thing I had to worry about was
painting, playing and learning my numbers and letters. And

not shoving crayons up my nose. What work could a five-year old do?

"Minty, what work could you do as a five-year old?"
"My job was to help Miss Susan take care of her brand new baby. I had to sleep on the floor and I was so homesick I cried all the time. But I didn't get much of a chance to sleep, because after I worked all day my main job was to keep the baby from crying at night. Whenever I couldn't get the baby to stop crying I was beaten with a whip. Once I was whipped five times even before breakfast."
"That's horrible."
"It never really got any better. After I got sent home from that job, they just kept sending me out year after year to work in white people's houses."
"How did you survive that?"
"The older I got, the smarter I got. I had one mistress who like to beat me every morning. So whenever I got dressed I would also put on extra clothes for padding, so the whipping wouldn't hurt so bad."

I just sat there in stunned silence and wondered what it would be like to be beaten every single day. I was amazed that even as a child, Harriet was already outsmarting her tormenters. She must have been very brave. I waited for Harriet to continue, but she just had a blank look on her face and stared out into the night sky. After a long time she started up again.

"I guess things finally got a little better when I turned twelve."
"What happened then?"
"I was old enough and strong enough to work in the fields. I liked that a lot better, because I liked working outside

and I was very strong. Strong enough to do a man's work."

I could see the sun starting to peep up over the sky. Harriet pulled on the reins and the horses slowly came to a stop. I nudged Noodles and he woke up and wiped the sleep slobber off his face.

"We're going to stop here and let the horses rest. We'll all get a little sleep, some food and start in again later on this afternoon."
"But Minty, I want to hear the rest of your story."
"Not now, Child, but maybe if you behave yourself I'll tell you how I found life's greatest gift."
"What's that?"
"Freedom."

"Minty"

Chapter 6
Holy Moses

After we hid the wagon off to the side of the road, Noodles magically pulled out some bedrolls and we bedded down for some shuteye. Even though my mind was full of Minty's story, I fell asleep immediately and slept like a rock. I woke up with a start with the full sun shining right in my eyes. I wiped my eyes and looked around. Good news: my swollen eye was definitely getting better. Bad news: no Noodles, no wagon, no Harriet, no nothing. If I wasn't in the middle of a field somewhere I might have thought I dreamt the whole thing. The sound of water running brought me back to reality.

I got up, stretched and walked toward the gurgling sound.

"Morning Miss Maddie."

I jumped. There in the middle of creek was Minty. Evidently she was taking a bath.

"Come on in the water's fine."
"I didn't exactly bring my swimming suit."
"Take it from me, you could use a bath."
"Where's Noodles?"
"Noodles left a couple of hours ago. He had to get the wagon back to Richmond."

I peeled off my disgusting clothes and slipped into the freezing cold creek. I was mad at Noodles for leaving without saying goodbye.

"So how are we going to get to Washington?"

"See those things on the end of your legs?"

"What?"

"Those would be your feet."

"Got it. How much farther do we have to go?"

"We are over half way there. If we get a move on I can get you there in a couple of days."

I made some quick calculations. Yesterday was April 10th, today was April 11th. I had to be in Washington before April 14th. I shivered in the cold creek. Even if we could make it, I wasn't going to have much time to change history. At least my rat bites were starting to heal up.

"So why do you like to be called 'Minty'?"

"My birth name was Araminta. My family always called me 'Minty.'"

"I thought your name was Harriet."

"I changed my name to 'Harriet' when I crossed over to freedom."

"I'm dying to hear all about that."

"Maybe later. We've got to get on up if we want to get to Washington. Last night I had a vision about President Lincoln."

"Really? What was it?"

"I'll tell you later. We need to move out."

As Minty turned to get out of the water I noticed the scars on her neck. Without thinking I reached out and touched the deep scars. She turned and held my hand and I could see tears in her eyes.

"Oh, Harriet."

"I told you it wasn't a pretty story."

"Does it - does it still hurt?"

"Only on the inside."

I wanted to say something else, but I couldn't find the words. We both slipped out of the creek and dried off without talking. Finally, Minty spoke.

"Okay, Maddie, here's the plan. You're going to wear this." She tossed me a very long and incredibly ugly dress.
"I don't know where you got those funny looking clothes, but you're going to blend in a lot better wearing these."
"Thanks, I guess." I slipped it on over my head.
"If anyone stops us, we have to pretend that you are my master's daughter and I am taking you back home. We're going to travel the back roads and try and stay away from people and out of trouble. If we're going to get you to Washington we'll have to travel some in the daylight. Keep your head low and your mouth shut."
"Okey dokey."
"One more thing. If you hear any dogs barking…"
"What?"
"Start running and try to keep up."

I looked at Minty to see if she was kidding, but it was clear she wasn't. I picked up my bedroll and rolled my clothes into a ball. Minty showed me how to carry them on my back. We stepped back out onto the road, looked both ways and started walking down the dusty road.

"I just can't believe Noodles left without even waking me up." I was missing him already.
"He's not too big on 'goodbyes'."
"I noticed."
"Oh, I almost forgot. He asked me to give you this. He said you might need it."

She tossed me something metal and I grabbed it out of the air as it spun end over end.

I looked it over. Whatever it was, it had a string attached to it.

"What is it?"
"Looks to be a whistle of some sort."

I blew it. Nothing. I blew it harder. Still no sound. Great. Leave it to Noodles to give me a whistle that didn't even work. I put the string around my neck and tucked it into my lovely dress. I scampered to catch up with Minty. She was getting on down the road.

We walked at a brisk pace. Every now and then we had to duck in the bushes to let people pass. Most of the people on the road were straggling soldiers wearing either blue or gray uniforms. They looked pretty pathetic no matter what side they were on. Sometimes the Union soldiers were more organized in patrols. Every now and then some shady looking characters, not in uniform, came riding by on horses. Whenever Minty saw them she made certain we hid really well.

"So can you tell me now how you got your freedom?"
"All right, but we have to keep our voices low."

She was almost whispering.

"Soon after I became a field hand I had some real bad luck. I was trying to protect one of my friends, another slave, from an angry overseer. We were inside a store and I tried to block the man from going outside after my friend.

Just at that moment he threw a weight after the other slave, but it ended up hitting me in the head."

"Ouch."

"It just about killed me. It broke my skull and drove part of my scarf into my head."

She pulled back the bandana she always wore on her head and showed me a terrible scar.

"I lay on a sickbed for months. I finally got better, but after that I started having spells."

"Spells?"

"I would black out without warning."

"How long did that last?"

"Oh, I still have them."

"Really?"

"They're not all bad though. That's when I have my visions."

"Visions?"

"Some people call them waking dreams. That's when I started dreaming about my freedom."

"Did you escape then?"

"No, it took me awhile to get the courage up to escape. Not too many women were successful at escaping. If you got caught you could be whipped to death. I got married and I didn't want to leave my husband and the rest of my family."

"How did you finally do it?"

"I was afraid my master was going to sell me further south where I would never have a chance to escape. So I finally took off in September, 1849."

"Was it hard?"

"It was so scary, but I had some help along the way. I gave a white woman a quilt I had made and she gave me a piece of paper with two names on it and directions to the next house. At the next house I gave another woman the paper and she gave me a broom and told me to start sweeping. I didn't understand at first, but then I realized she wanted me to act like just another working slave. When her husband came home he hid me in a wagon and took me to the next station."

"What did the paper say?"

"I don't know, Maddie. I never learned how to read. I had to rely on the kindness of strangers. They were very brave. If they would have been caught with a fugitive slave they would have been arrested."

"Were you ever alone?"

"I was alone most of the time. I traveled at night, followed the streams north and hid in hollow trees during the daytime. I wasn't afraid though. I was living my dream. My dream to fly away to freedom. It took me a couple of weeks, but I finally made it to Philadelphia."

"But you went back to rescue other slaves, right?"

"Many times, but that's enough talking for now."

The sun started to go down and I noticed how hungry I was. I hadn't really eaten for two days except that bread Noodles gave me.

"Minty, I hate to bother you, but I could use a little something to eat."

"Down the road a piece we'll stop and try to find some vittles."

We walked a little farther and crept around to the back of a farmhouse. Minty climbed the steps and quietly knocked on the door. A white woman came to the door. She was frowning.

"I already told them soldiers we don't have any food. Now

get yourself along before I get out my gun."

Suddenly she stopped talking and her mouth dropped open.

"Oh my goodness! Moses, is that you? Can it really be you after all these years?"

She practically leaped out the door and gave Minty a big bear hug. Harriet gave me a wink and a smile and I knew then we would have plenty to eat for dinner that night.

DISTANCE BETWEEN RICHMOND AND
WASHINGTON CITY IS ABOUT 100 MILES

Chapter 7
The Hunted

I didn't really realize how hungry I was until we sat down to eat. I ate so much I almost passed out. Biscuits, ham, gravy, mashed potatoes, some green stuff I didn't recognize and even apple pie for dessert. Yum, yum, yum. I wish I could tell you what Harriet talked about with our host, but I was too busy eating. I only heard an occasional word or two. I know I should have been listening, but the eating machine just took over.

Every now and then, Minty and "the world's greatest cook" would burst out laughing and they would laugh so hard, tears would come to their eyes. I kept hearing words like "slave catcher", "raids", "bounty" "Harper's Ferry", and "John Brown". Then I got it. This had to be one of the stops on the old Underground Railroad. They were telling war stories about their adventures just like when my dad gets together with his brothers and sisters. I finally stopped eating and tried to listen, but about three seconds after I stopped stuffing my face with food I started getting really sleepy. I found a bedroom, a nice soft bed and then the sleeping machine took over.

I didn't wake until Harriet shook me.

"Maddie, time to go."

I stretched and yawned. It would have been so much easier to sleep a few more hours. Or days. Who knew changing history would involve so much sleep deprivation? I shuffled out of bed and followed Harriet into the kitchen. We said goodbye to our host and left through the back door. It was already dark and I was still sleepy, so I just followed without talking.

Two full days were gone since I "landed" in Richmond. That meant I only had two more days to get to Washington and put my plan into action. Actually, I didn't really have a plan, but I tried not to think about that too much. It was a beautiful warm night with a full moon and sky full of stars. I started humming and even skipping a little bit. I felt so happy I burst into a song.

Minty grabbed me by the arm and put a finger to her lips.

"What's the matter, Harriet, you don't like, 'She'll Be Comin' Around the Mountain'?"
"Maddie, it is very important that we keep quiet."
"Who's going to be out this late at night?"

That's when we heard the horses. Harriet took off like a shot and I tried my best to keep up. We were at a point in the road where it was mostly farmland, so there was absolutely no place to hide. It was only a few seconds before the horsemen caught up to us. The three men on horseback looked like a rough bunch. They weren't soldiers, but one of them was wearing a Confederate Cap. The leader pulled up his horse and gave us a big grin. This "winner" had about three teeth.

"Well, well, well. Whatta we have here, fellas? Looks like a couple of runaways."

I tried to remember what Harriet told me to say if we were stopped. I struggled to come up with something.

"Uh, sir, this is my sister and we are on our way to the, uh, market."

The leader jumped off his horse and got right up into my face. This guy hadn't had a bath since the war started.

"Kinda late to be headin' to the market, ain't it? And I'm purty shur this'n ain't your sister unless you got some Negro blood in ya."

He laughed like a donkey, and grabbed me by the back of the hair.

"Now, I'm gonna give you one more chance to tell me the truth. It's just a little dangerous 'round here this time of night and I'd hate for youins to get yourselves in trouble. Looks ta me like this here might be a runaway slave that needs ta be returned to its master."

I just stared at him in disbelief, and then I lost it.

"Hey, toothless, I've got a news flash for you! In case you haven't noticed, the war is over and the South lost! All of the slaves are now free and you and your kind will have to do their own work for a change. So just let go of me and you and your redneck friends can be on your way."

I glanced over at Minty and couldn't help but notice the frown she had on her face. She was looking right at me and slowly shaking her head from side to side. Johnny Reb wannabe gripped my hair tighter and I heard a low growl that made my skin crawl.

"Maybe I should just cut your throat right now."

The next thing I know, out of nowhere, Harriet whips out a pistol and fires it into the air.

The noise shocked everyone and while they were staring at her I made my move. I grabbed old Toothless by the arm, bit him and twisted free. I stomped on his foot and slapped his horse on the butt as I went running by. The horse, frightened by the gunshot and the whipping, took off like a shot. Minty and I took off just as fast in the other direction. It wasn't easy running in that long dress, but I was pretty motivated. We jumped a fence, headed across a field and didn't stop until we reached the safety of the trees.

"Maddie, Maddie, Maddie."

Harriet was clearly not happy. She had the same look on her face that my Dad did when he found me brushing the dog's teeth with his toothbrush.

"It's ok, Minty. They'll never be able to catch us in here with their horses. The forest is too thick."

She started to say something, and then she stopped, cocked her head and listened intently.

"You hear that?"
"I don't hear a thing."
"Listen."

That's when I heard the unmistakable sound of barking off in the distance. Harriet had a look of pure terror on her face. The hounds were loose. I realized that Minty probably still had a bounty on her head from her days as a conductor on the URR. If she fell into the wrong hands she would probably be hanged. I had put both of us into terrible jeopardy.

We sprinted into the woods with the baying of the hounds echoing in our ears. It didn't take Minty long to open her bag of tricks. After we ran awhile, she stopped and pulled me to the ground. She frantically pulled some plants from the ground and thrust them at me.

"Quick, rub these on your feet."
"What is it?" I wrinkled my nose at the smell.
"It's asafetida - it will put the dogs off our trail."

She was up and running by the time I finished one foot.

"Which way, Minty?"
"Just follow that star and try to keep up."
"What star?"
"The North Star."

We changed directions many times, switching back over and over, trying to lose the dogs. We climbed up trees and jumped off the limbs. We criss-crossed streams and creeks. We ran up shallow streams and jumped from rock to rock. I was running out of steam. We swam across a small pond. My dress was soaking wet and it was getting harder and harder to keep up with Minty. She finally stopped and I doubled over in pain, gasping for air.

"What if we get separated, Minty?"
"Just find the road and head north. Follow the star."

We started moving again when we heard the bloodhounds excitedly barking. They once more picked up our scent and we were off and running. That's when I noticed it was beginning to rain. Our clear, moonlit night had suddenly grown dark and foreboding. The hounds kept coming.

The rain made the ground slick and I kept slipping and falling. I did my best to keep up with Harriet, but the darkness and the rain made it harder and harder to keep her in sight.

My wet dress kept getting caught in the bushes and thorns, and I had to tear myself loose more than once. I burst into a clearing just in time to see Minty leaving the other side. The rain kept falling and the baying of the pack made me wonder how they were keeping our scent in the rain. I kept pounding forward. I reached the edge of the clearing, and took another tumble into a puddle. When I looked up I saw five dogs burst into the clearing barking their fool heads off.

"HARRIET! HARRIET! HARRIET!"

No answer. I pulled myself out of the mud and just started running with the hounds in hot pursuit. No way was I going to outrun them. At best I had about a minute's head start. It's funny how things pop into your head when you are desperate.

"Hey, Maggie."
"Dad, I'm busy."
"I wouldn't exactly call playing Playstation being busy."
"And…?"
"I picked up some books for you to read." Dad tossed them on my bed.
'Five Boys in a Cave', 'My Side of the Mountain', and 'Where the Red Fern Grows'. Great, Dad, these books are all about boys. How come you never bring me books about girls?"
"They're not just about boys. They're about people struggling to solve their problems and overcoming adversity. Got something against boys, anyway?"

"They smell, they're annoying and worst of all they dress funny."

"Prove it."

"Ok, for instance, Dad, that is the third day in a row you have worn the exact same shirt and pants that, by the way, do NOT match. I'm going to call a press conference when you actually change your clothes."

"No fair using me as an example."

"Ok, how about the guy in my class who named his pencils, 'Larry and Mojingles'?"

"Alright, you have me on that one. How about this? I'll give you $5 for each of the books you read. If you don't think they're great you can keep the money. If they are, you have to give me the money back."

Four days later I sadly left the fifteen bucks on his dresser. Dad was pretty good at picking out interesting books, even if they were about boys.

Anyway as I was trying to escape from the pack of dogs, I realized that the characters in those books never panicked. What I needed was a plan. Even though I couldn't outrun the barking maniacs, if I got to a deep enough river I might be able to out swim them. I couldn't believe I was actually hoping for another river. I must be out of my mind.

I took a hard right and kept on chugging along. The dogs were relentless and getting closer by the second. When I saw the river ahead of me, I couldn't believe my luck. Just a few steps more and I would make it. I was just starting to go into my dive when the first dog pulled me down. At first it shocked me, because I hadn't heard this dog bark. He must have sneaked up on me. "Fido" had a good hold on my dress and I went down like a ton of bricks. We went skidding along together for a few feet and then the rest of his pals arrived. I made a desperate charge for the water, but they blocked my path. I suddenly realized they weren't going to kill me. They just wanted to corner me, until their masters arrived. It was really hard to think with "crazy dog" ripping my dress to shreds, but I needed a new plan. The lunatic dog finally tore off the bottom half of my dress, so I was actually free for a few seconds. I did a three sixty and noticed I was standing next to a huge oak tree. I jumped for a branch, kicked one of those yelping suckers in the mouth and managed to hold on, even with the pack jumping and scratching and biting my legs. I pulled myself up by my elbows and scrambled up a few branches.

The dogs below were going absolutely bananas. They must have thought they treed the biggest coon in the history of hunting with dogs. They probably thought they were going to be inducted into the "Idiot Barking Dog Hall of Fame." I just wanted to kill every last one of them. My plan wasn't working out too well. I figured I had about two minutes before "Toothless and the Morons" arrived. As my dad would say, this was a "complete disaster."

What the heck. I pulled out Noodles' whistle and blew it with all my might. Suddenly the dogs stopped barking. They whimpered a couple of times and then lay down. NOODLES COMES THROUGH! I wriggled to the end of the branch, dropped into the cold water and started floating down the river trying to put as much distance between me and my hunters as possible.

Chapter 8
Harriet, The Spy

I didn't stay in the river for long. It was freezing cold, and I floated and swam as long as I could before I hauled myself out. Since I lost my sense of direction running from the dogs, I had no idea where I was. What's new? I tried finding the North Star like Minty said, but the clouds made the night sky pitch black. I had to get moving though, because I wasn't certain I was rid of the dogs once and for all and I was shivering from the cold. I knew I could warm up if I started moving. Then I remembered another trick Minty taught me.

I found the closest tree and felt all around it for moss. Minty told me moss only grows on the north side of trees, so I found the moss and headed out in that direction. Every few minutes or so I checked a tree, felt for the moss and stayed on course. It was tough picking my way through the forest in the dark, but I knew that sooner or later I would run into the road. I must have been in the woods for an hour or two when I finally found it. I hoped it was the road we were on before we got separated, but I had no way of knowing if I was right.

I gave the hoot owl call Minty told me to use as a signal if we lost each other. Nothing. I started up the road, taking care to keep my eyes and ears open for any sign of people, horses or rabid dogs. I walked the rest of the night, until the pink and orange light of dawn spread across the eastern sky. I tried my owl call a few more times with no luck.

I began to worry that I had lost Harriet for good. How far was it to Washington?

The morning light reminded me that another day had gone by. Today was April 13th. I only had one more day to get to Washington and save President Lincoln. Time was running out. What I really needed was a telephone. It would be a heck of a lot easier just to phone ahead, and let everybody know what was going to happen. There were only a few slight problems with that plan. I didn't have a cell phone, there were no phone booths anywhere and PHONES HADN'T BEEN INVENTED YET. Duh.

Suddenly that little light switch in my brain flipped on. That was it. Phone booth. Booth. BOOTH! It all came back to me. John Wilkes Booth was the person who murdered Abraham Lincoln. All I had to do was get to Washington, find John Wilkes Booth, and stop him cold. I wasn't as discouraged anymore. I picked up the pace and tried to stop thinking about how hungry I was.

The sound of voices ahead of me brought me back to reality. I fled the road and ducked behind some bushes. It took me a couple of minutes to realize the voices weren't getting any closer. Whoever was making this noise was pretty much staying in one place. I emerged out of the bushes and carefully moved toward the sound. I stayed close to the edge of the road and crept closer to the commotion.

When I finally got close enough to the noise, what I saw shocked and surprised me. It was easy enough for me to realize I had stumbled upon a military camp. The tents, soldiers and campfires were a dead giveaway. That's not the part that blew me away though. This camp had both Confederates and Yankees in it. These soldiers were not at war. They were laughing, joking and playing what had to be BASEBALL. That's right. The War was over and these former enemies were just having some fun. Dad would

NEVER believe that they were playing baseball during the Civil War. It wasn't exactly the game I knew, but they were pitching, hitting, running and cheering just like baseball players would be doing for the next 150 years. Unbelievable.

I watched the game for awhile, but I kept getting distracted by an owl that was hooting nearby. The guy on second base looked vaguely familiar. Hoot, hoot, hoot. Somebody must have forgotten to tell this dopey bird that owls do not hoot in the daytime. I tried to follow the game, but the hooting just kept getting louder. I was about to throw a rock in the direction of the bird, when I saw Minty grinning at me through the foliage. She put a finger to her lips and signaled for me to follow her.

When we got out of earshot, she started laughing so hard I thought someone would hear her. She gave me a big hug, and we laughed until we fell down.

"Maddie, I don't think you'd make a very good conductor."
"Why not?"
"I've never hooted so loud for so long my whole life."
"Sorry, I was kinda caught up in the game."
"I'm so glad you made it. Did you have a little trouble with the dogs?"
"That would be an understatement. I finally shook them though. What about you?"

We both shared our escape stories and then Minty said we had to get moving. She took one look at my torn clothes and told me to wait. I wasn't too keen on getting separated again, but waited patiently. She came back a few minutes with my bundled clothes and some food. I thought for sure my clothes had been lost, but somehow she had managed to keep them. I changed into my warm clothes and greedily gobbled up the biscuits and gravy she offered. She also handed me a blue army cap.

"Here, put this on. We'll probably have better luck the rest of the way if we dress like men. I think we can pass you off as a boy."

Terrific. Do I have to scratch myself and spit too? I put my hair under the cap, and started following Harriet back to the road. We slipped by the encampment unnoticed and kept on the path to Washington. We passed several people on the road, and I was surprised to notice that we were not nearly as cautious as we had been.

"What's up, Minty? Why aren't we hiding like we were?"
"Two reasons. We're not far from Washington, so it's safer now and we're running out of time. Don't you have to be there by tomorrow?"
"Right."

As the day went by, we saw more and more soldiers. Soldiers from both sides were going in both directions. Many of them were wounded. All of them though carried the same worn out, hollowed-eyed expression. They looked exhausted and you couldn't really tell which side had won. I tried not to stare, but they were very different from the soldiers I had seen in Richmond. These guys were beaten up and beaten down. They looked like they just wanted to get home. No wonder some of them stopped to have a little fun playing baseball.

"Hey, Minty."
"What?"
"What's up with the gun?"
"Don't you know soldiers always carry their guns with

them?"

"What do you mean, soldier?"

"You didn't know I was a soldier, Maddie?"

"Are you kidding me?"

"Never."

I had to hear this. I wanted to hear more about Harriet's amazing life.

"So after you escaped to Philadelphia why didn't you just stay there?"

"I did stay for awhile. I found a job and worked to pay my way, but I was really lonely and missing my kinfolk."

"So you went back to the place where you had been a slave?"

"Yes I did, but I was very careful not to get caught. The first trip back I rescued my niece, Kizzy, and her two daughters. They were about to be sold further south. The next spring I went back again and brought out my brother and two other men."

"You weren't afraid you would get caught?"

"Of course I was, but with every trip I gained more and more confidence. I always used God and my visions to guide me."

I thought about this for awhile. I began to realize what an extraordinary person Minty was. It was weird the way every now and then she would stop talking and just stare off into space for a few minutes. My dad gets a dumb look like that on his face every once in awhile, but he's not having a vision - he's just passing gas.

"So that's how you became a conductor on the Underground Railroad?"

"Yes, back in '51 I committed to the UGRR. They would

sponsor my trips with money and contacts. I started making about two trips a year. I usually made my trips in the winter when the nights were longer. I worked all spring and summer to raise money for the raids."

"How did you know where to go? How did the slaves know you were coming to get them?"

"The UGRR had safe houses all along the way where we could hide or be fed. Many of the people who helped us were Quakers or abolitionists. Sometimes we would know that certain slaves wanted to be free. I would go to an area and spread the word about when and where the escape would take place."

"Did you have any close calls?"

"Many. The bigger the group, the more dangerous the trips. I took as many as 25 slaves at a time. Eventually I was able to bring all of my family out including my parents. I got everybody out except one."

"Who didn't make it?"

"I went back to get my husband. I found out he had remarried and he didn't want to go. He wouldn't even see me."

I kept quiet for a few minutes. I had forgotten that Minty was married. That must have been so hard for her. She risked her life to rescue her husband, but he found someone else and wouldn't even talk to her. What a bum. Harriet started talking again.

"Things got so dangerous I had to start carrying a gun."

"Did you ever have to shoot it?"

"Only every now and then. I used it most to threaten the people I was trying to get out. They would get so scared, sometimes I had to point the gun at them to get them moving. It came in handy once for something else, though."

"What happened?"
"I was on a smuggling trip and I got this crazy infection in my mouth. I put up with the pain as long as I could, then I knocked my teeth out with the gun to stop the pain."

I winced just thinking about that. So that's how Harriet lost her top row of teeth. Ouch.

"How many trips did you end up making?"
"Too many to count."
"How many slaves did you help escape?"
"Hundreds. I never counted them."
"Why did you stop?"
"I was getting too famous. They had wanted posters for me everywhere offering rewards for my capture."
"How much?"
"Anywhere from $15,000 to $40,000."

I tried to think how much that was worth in the 1850's. Probably a lot. A whole lot.

"That's why you stopped?"
"I wasn't afraid. I didn't want to stop, but all the other folks in the UGRR said I would be more useful raising money. I started going around making speeches all over, telling everyone about my trips and narrow escapes. We used the money to help many other slaves escape and to fight against slavery."
"So you became famous?"
"I suppose. But I would have rather been making the raids. That's why I was so happy when the war started."
"Is that when you became a soldier?"
"Not at first. In the beginning I was a volunteer nurse. When the army figured out that I could travel around the

south without being noticed, they made me into a soldier and then later I talked them into letting me be a spy."

"Minty, you were a spy!?"

"Sure. I knew my way around every back road, river, plantation and city all over Virginia and South Carolina. My ten years as a conductor on the Underground Railroad came in handy."

Every hour I spent with Minty was more and more amazing. I never knew she was a soldier or a spy. This was the most incredible story I had ever heard. You couldn't make this stuff up even if you wanted to.

"Tell me about some of your spying adventures."

'Want to hear about the Combahee River Raid?"

"Absolutely."

"In June of '63 we infiltrated and mapped out South Carolina near the sea island coast. This was one of the strongholds of the south. Those slave owners were some of the richest and most stubborn in the whole Confederacy. One night around midnight we headed upriver with three boats loaded with 150 black soldiers."

"There were black soldiers?"

"Of course. Remind me to tell you about Colonel Robert Gould Shaw and the Fightin' Fifty-Fourth."

"Ok. What happened next?"

"I guided the troops upriver past the Rebel torpedoes. At designated spots along the river we met up with slaves from the plantations who wanted to be free."

"How did they know where to meet you?"

"I had spread the word on scouting expeditions. I never saw such a sight. More than 750 slaves escaped that night. Quite a few pigs and chickens too. After we got the slaves on board, the soldiers robbed the warehouses and set the huge mansions on fire. By the time the Rebs figured out what we were doing it was too late. By the morning light when they finally fired on us, we were out of range."

"That is awesome. Tell me more."

I hadn't noticed with all our walking and talking that night had fallen.

"I'll tell you more later. Right now we need to find some vittles and a place to sleep. You wait here and I'll be back in a little while with some food. We're almost to Washington. You need to rest up for your big day tomorrow."

While Harriet was gone I sat down and rested my head against a tree. My mind was full of the incredible tales that Minty told me. She was absolutely the bravest person I had ever met. I hoped I could be as brave tomorrow.

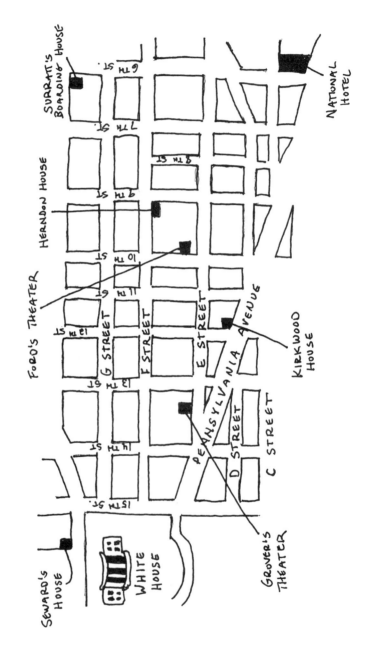

WASHINGTON CITY, 1865

Surratt's Boarding House
National Hotel
Herndon House
Ford's Theater
Kirkwood House
Seward's House
White House
Grover's Theater
G Street
F Street
E Street
Pennsylvania Avenue
D Street
C Street
6th St.
7th St.
8th St.
9th St.
10th St.
11th St.
12th St.
13th St.
14th St.
15th St.

Chapter 9
Washington City

It didn't take long for Minty to return. When she got back she had a satchel full of food: bread, turkey, milk and even an apple. It had been a long time since our last meal at the farmhouse, so I really chowed down. She told me she got the food from a Union encampment nearby. Her military connections were helping out big time.

"Maddie, I'm going to have to be leaving you soon."

My mouth dropped opened. I assumed all along Harriet was going to help me. This was a big shock.

"What? Why?"
"I have to get back to my regiment. I've already been gone too long. Now that the war's over I need to get back to my family."
"But I can't do this by myself. I don't know anything about Washington. Please, Minty, you've got to help me."
"I'm sorry, child. You are going to have to fight this battle on your own. My vision only showed me to take you to Washington City."

I had never heard anyone call it that. I guess they started calling it Washington D.C. later on.

"Don't you want me to help save President Lincoln?" I was practically begging now.
"That's funny. You know I wasn't always such a big

supporter of old Honest Abe. I never thought he was doing enough to help the Negroes. But after the Emancipation Proclamation I really grew to admire and to love him."

"So that means you will help me?"
"I'm sorry, Maddie. I've got to go where my visions tell me to go. When you wake up tomorrow I'll probably be gone."
"No, no, NO!" I was starting to cry. Wait a minute.
"Minty, what did your dream tell you about me? Am I going to..."

Harriet was deep in one of her trances. She came out of it a few minutes later, but I could tell her mind was made up. After we finished our meal, we got our bedrolls and found a comfortable place to sleep. Even though I knew I needed a good night's sleep to have any chance tomorrow, I wanted to hear more about Minty's fabulous life. On and on into the night we talked. She told me about some amazing people and events that I never heard of: William Still, Sojourner Truth, Harper's Ferry, William Seward, Gettysburg, John Brown, Frederick Douglas, the Battle of Bull Run and Robert Gould Shaw. I tried desperately to stay awake, but my eyelids just kept slamming shut. The last thing I remember was falling asleep with Minty's arm around me.

I woke up with a start, just as the pink dawn was lighting up the Eastern sky. Minty was gone. She must have slipped away just like she told me she would. I was surprised to find when I opened my hand, it held two silver dollars. I whispered "thanks" to Minty. She must have thought I might need some money in Washington City. I stretched and rubbed the sleep out of my eyes. I found a nearby pond and washed my face and hair. Time for an assessment. I felt pretty good. My reflection in the water showed that my eye was still black, but not too swollen. The rat bites were mostly scabbed over and were starting to itch a little. I had a good night's rest and even though I was a little hungry, I wasn't starving. Time to move out.

I dried my hair the best I could, put it under my hat and started hunting for the road. In a few seconds I was on my way to Washington City. As usual I had no idea of what I was going to do when I got there. First things first.

Even though it was early, there was plenty of traffic. It was a cool, misty morning and I was happy to have the military coat Minty had left for me. I followed a column of soldiers and tried to blend in. I had learned from Harriet to keep my head down and my mouth shut. The last thing I wanted to do was draw attention to myself.

As we got closer to the city I began to focus on the job I had ahead of me. I really didn't have a good plan, but I figured the first thing I needed to do was to find my way around. I had been to Washington, D.C. once with my mom when I was very little, but I didn't remember much about it.

As I crossed the bridge over the Potomac River into the city I was impressed with all the activity. Even though it was still early in the morning there were all kinds of people up and about conducting their business. The iron-wheeled wagons thundered over the cobblestones. Women in hooped skirts bustled along the wooden sidewalks. There were pigs, chickens and ducks scattered everywhere you looked. There were soldiers everywhere. It wasn't going to be hard blending into a city this busy. What wasn't going to be easy was finding Booth.

I started to concentrate all my brainpower on Booth. I

tried to remember all I could about him. The only things that kept popping into my head were that he was an actor and the shooting was going to take place at Ford's Theater. Other than that, I didn't have much to go on. Suddenly I saw a landmark that I recognized. Looming over the horizon was the Washington Monument and a little further on what had to be the Capitol Building. My limited knowledge of history was paying off. I knew the White House couldn't be far from those places. When I got closer I asked a stranger where to find the White House. He pointed the way and I made my way along Pennsylvania Avenue.

In a few minutes I was standing in front of the White House. It didn't look anything like I remembered in the history books or on television. In fact it looked a little shabby and run-down. I guess there wasn't enough money to keep it looking spiffy with the war and all. There was already plenty of activity at the White House. Lots of people were coming and going, but they all had to pass through a guard gate and get permission from the soldiers there. I thought about trying to get to see President Lincoln, but I vividly remembered the incident with the soldiers in Richmond and I definitely did NOT want to go through that again. If the soldiers thought I knew something about the President being assassinated they might throw me in jail. Then my mission would be a complete and total failure. I decided the best plan of action for the moment was to try and find Booth. He had to be around here somewhere if he was going to commit murder that night. Maybe if I found him, I could talk him out of it, or at least slow him down a little.

I stared hard at the dozens of people passing by. Which one of these jokers was Booth? I had absolutely no way of knowing. I had to find someone who knew Booth and could tell me where he was or at least what he looked like. One hour of my precious day had already gone by. I didn't have any time to waste. I finally decided to try and find Ford's Theater. Maybe someone there could help me. I mustered up my deepest voice and asked a well dressed woman walking by.

"Excuse me Ma'am. I'm new in Washington City and don't know my way around too well. Can you tell me how to get to Ford's Theater from here?"
"You mean Ford's Opera House?"
"I guess that's it."
"It's not far. Just walk down G Street four or five blocks and then take a right on 10th street. After about a block and a half it should be on the right."
"Much obliged Ma'am."

I tipped my hat and all my hair came tumbling out. Der. Fortunately the lady either didn't notice or care, because she just kept walking. I wouldn't make a very good spy with numb-skull moves like that. I was going to have to be a lot more careful if I was going to catch Booth. I hurriedly made my way down G Street.

FORD'S THEATER

JWB

Chapter 10
Star Spangled Assassin

It didn't take me long to reach Ford's Opera House. It was easy to find by all the advertisements plastered outside. There was one that caught my eye: FORD'S THEATER, FRIDAY EVENING, APRIL 14TH, 1865, LAST NIGHT of LAURA KEENE in OUR AMERICAN COUSIN. I looked around and climbed the steps. Naturally the door was locked, so I started looking for a doorbell. Nothing. I pounded on the door for about ten minutes before some sleepy looking guy opened it.

"Sorry, fella, the box office doesn't open until noon."
"Actually I was looking for Mr. Booth."
"Which one?"
"There's more than one?'
"Sure, Edwin, Junius and John Wilkes."

That was news to me, but that last name rang a bell.

"John Wilkes, I think. Is he the one who hangs around
   here?'
"That would be him. But I haven't seen him today." He
   started to close the door.

I stuck my foot in the door.

 "Do you know where I can find him?"
"Check around back. Ned might know where he is."
"Ned?"
"Ned Spangler. Come back later if you want to buy a
   ticket."

As the door closed behind me I thought that might not be a bad idea. If I couldn't find Booth today I would definitely need to get into the theater tonight. I hurried around the building, but didn't find anything except a couple of horses in a stable. I waited for a few minutes not sure of what to do next. Finally some scruffy looking guy came out of the stable. I approached him.

"Are you Ned Spangler?"

He eyed me suspiciously.

"Maybe I am and maybe I ain't. Who wants to know?"

Great, another genius. I was losing patience.

"Whoever you are I'm looking for John Wilkes Booth. Do you know where I can find him?"
"I might if the price is right. What do you want with Booth?"
"Uh, uh…"

I struggled before I thought of something.

"I'm a big fan and I wanted to meet the great actor."
"Cost you a dollar."

I fished around in my pocket and gave him one of my two dollars. This better be good.

"He lives a few blocks from here at the National Hotel. I ain't seen him this morning, but he usually gets his hair cut and a shave at Booker and Stewart's Barbershop on E Street. He's probably done gone from there though. If he ain't there try the National."

He turned and walked away.

"Let me warn you though, kid. He don't take too kindly
to Yankee soldiers. But if yer real nice he might
give you his autograph."

Yeah, I thought. I want the autograph of one of the most
hated men in history. What I really wanted was to take his
name OUT of the history books.

I spent the rest of the day chasing John Wilkes Booth.
Everywhere I went it seemed as though I just missed him. I
went to the barbershop, the National Hotel, Surratt's Boarding
House, back to Ford's Theater, a different stable, Herndon
House, back to Surratt's and finally Kirkwood House. At each
place they had seen Booth, or they expected him to be back,
but they didn't know exactly where he was. Time was
running out. I was frustrated, tired and hungry. At least I was
getting to know my way around Washington City. I also found
out two things.

First, everyone was in a great mood because the war was
over. From the hotels to the stables to the saloons every single
person I ran into was either drunk or overjoyed that the war
was finally over. I spent another nickel on a newspaper and
read some grim war statistics. The Washington Evening Star
estimated that almost 600,000 men from both sides had died
from the war. I couldn't comprehend that. The only good
news was that almost 4,000,000 slaves had been freed.
Something else in the paper caught my eye. There was an
announcement that President Lincoln and Mrs. Lincoln would
be attending Ford's Theater that night along with General
Ulysses S. Grant. Another fact I didn't know. At least I was
on the right track, but I had to find Booth.

Second, John Wilkes Booth was incredibly popular. Apparently JWB was well known and well liked. It didn't seem strange to anyone that he might have a fan like me following him all around the city just trying to get a glimpse of the famous actor. If they only knew what he was up to, they wouldn't think he was so terrific. I was tempted a couple of times to warn people about his plan, but I decided to stick to my strategy of finding Booth and confronting him myself. If I ran out of time I could always tell my story.

Someone told me to look for Booth at Grover's Theater. That was the other theater over by the White House I was told. Another long walk across Washington City. It sure would have been a lot easier just to get on the internet and track him down on dirtyrottencriminals.com. What I needed was a cab or at least a cell phone. The only technology I had available to me was on the ends of my legs. And those "dogs" were barking.

Of course when I got to Grover's, Booth had just left. No, they didn't know where he was going. I was exhausted and starving to death. I decided I needed to get something to eat, so I wouldn't pass out. The clock on the corner said it was 4:15. I didn't want to stop, but I knew I needed to refuel. Deery's Tavern was above the theater, so I trudged up the steps, pushed open the squeaky door and sat down. I spent another quarter on a meal of steak, eggs, grits and some green tea.

That was one well spent quarter. With a full belly, I thought about my next move. Three choices: I had to find Booth OR tell someone what I knew OR go to Ford's Theater myself tonight. I was thinking over my options when a strange feeling came over me. Then I saw something that shocked me back into reality and took my breath away. Goose bump alert.

At the bar with his back to me was a man with jet black hair wearing a fancy coat and tan riding boots. I stared at him for a couple of minutes. When he brought his drink up to his mouth I noticed his left wrist had a tattoo. The letters were unmistakable. "J". "W." "B". I finally found my man. I caught my breath, summoned my courage and walked over and sat down at the bar next to him. I held my hands tight to keep from shaking.

"Say aren't you John Wilkes Booth?"

He turned to me.

His eyes were liquid pools of blue and his hair and features were striking.

He gave me a polite smile, and slightly bowed.

"That I am, young man, that I am. How may I be of service?"

I sat there with my mouth open like a doofus. I don't know what I expected, but Booth was definitely not the evil monster I imagined. It hardly seemed possible that this handsome young man was going to try and murder the President in a few short hours. He stared at me for a couple of seconds, picked up his hat and started to leave. My big chance to change history and I was blowing it.

"Wait, Mr. Booth!"
"Yes?" He hesitated.
"Can I buy you a drink or something? I'd really like to talk to you for a second."
"Sorry, good fellow. I've got a busy evening ahead."

He turned to go.

"But I want to talk to you about... about... about the war."
I saw his eyes flash a little and his face darkened."
"What about it? You should be elated with your victory."

He was practically growling.

"But now that the war's over we should all just try to get
along, right?"
"I doubt that will be possible."
"We can do it."

He sneered.

"Not with that great ape in the White House."
"He was just trying to the keep the country together."

Booth's voice rose.

"NOW he plans to give the SLAVES the right to vote.
This country was formed for the WHITE, not for the
black man. It will not stand. I will not abide it."

This wasn't going too well. I was just getting him all riled
up. I tried to change the subject.

"Mr. Booth, you are my all-time favorite actor."

He pulled me close and I could smell the alcohol on his
breath. His eyes were blazing and his hand pulled back his
jacket for me to see. I gasped at the derringer tucked inside
his vest.

"After today, my friend, I will be the most famous actor in all of history."

I couldn't help myself. I stared right back at him. He was definitely scary. All the earlier politeness drained out of our conversation.

I whispered back,

"I know what you're planning, Booth. It's not going to happen."

He laughed.

"You going to stop me, schoolboy? Say, are you the person who's been following me around all day, trying to get a glimpse of the famous John Wilkes Booth?"

I pulled him in even closer.

"You-are-not-going-to-kill-President Lincoln."

The ends of his moustache curled up and a smile spread slowly across his face. It was the most evil smile I had ever seen in all my life. He jerked away, picked up his top hat and turned to go. I stood up, lunged and grabbed his arm. In one swift movement he whirled and kicked my legs out from under me. I landed hard on my backside and it knocked the wind out of me. I was gasping for air as I saw him leaving out the door. He turned and pointed at me.

He hissed,

"Last warning. Do not meddle in affairs that do not concern you. I won't be so accommodating next time."

In an instant his coattails flapped out the door. He was gone. I struggled to my feet, but by the time I got down the stairs Booth was nowhere to be seen. I sprinted up the street, but there was no sign of the wicked assassin. Terrific. I found myself on G Street where a crowd formed.

As I stood there a black carriage flanked by soldiers on horseback came riding by. The tall, elegant person riding in the back was unmistakable. There, right in front of my eyes was President Abraham Lincoln taking a late afternoon carriage ride. He smiled and waved and I froze with my mouth wide open. As he passed by, the sad, tired eyes of Lincoln stared out at me from his hollow face. I waved back at him and smiled, but my heart was full of hopeless desperation. The President would be dead in just a few hours if I didn't do something fast. I looked at the clock on the corner and noticed the sunlight was beginning to fade. 5:00. No sign of Booth, no plan and precious little time. Tick. Tick. Tick.

Chapter 11
Conspiracy Theory

I desperately looked everywhere for Booth, but there was no sign of the scoundrel. I finally decided to head back to Ford's Theater to buy a ticket. I barely noticed the scent of spring lilacs or the carriage wheels crunching on the gravel road. When I got to Ford's, there was a short line at the box office. The thought crossed my mind that since both Lincoln and Grant were scheduled to appear, that they might sell out of tickets. To my relief there were a few seats left. I plunked down my fifty cents and looked the ticket over.

"Excuse me, sir. I've never been to Ford's Theater before. Do you think I can come in and take a look at my seat?"
"Sorry, not today, soldier. Everyone's busy getting ready for the President, so there's no one to show you around."

I was going to argue, but the clerk was already busy with other customers, so I decided to give him a break. I absolutely had to get in the theater though, to look around and get my bearings. I walked around to the alley in the back and looked for Ned Spangler. Sure enough, there he was sitting on a barrel drinking whiskey straight out of the bottle. Nice.

"Hey, Ned. I want to get a tour of the theater. You know anybody who can show me around?"
"You again?"

He snorted.

"I probably could since I work there and all, but I'm taking a break right now. Maybe Johnny Peanut can give you the grand tour. Got any money left?"

I felt in my pocket. I only had twenty cents left.

"Would he do it for a dime?"
"He might. But you're gonna have to wait a few minutes."

I just stood there for awhile and Ned finally banged on the back door and Johnny Peanut came out. He wasn't too bright, but he was nice enough and agreed to show me around for a dime. I pretended I wanted to find my seat, but what I really wanted was to get a look at the box where President Lincoln would be sitting. He said that wasn't allowed, but he could show me the outside.

The "Presidential Box" was pretty impressive. It was to the right of the stage directly overlooking the play. It was draped with flags and had a big picture of George Washington right in the middle of the back wall. When I asked Johnny Peanut how to get in, he led me to the second floor of seats. He said this was the "Dress Circle" and these were some of the best seats in the house, but if I wanted to catch a glimpse of Old Abe tonight the best place was the ground floor. He showed me the little white door that led to the box and the chair outside where the guard sat when the President came to the theater.

"Thanks a lot, Mr. Peanut."
"You are welcome. It's kinda funny though."
"What's that?"

"Yer not the first person who's been snoopin' 'round this box today."
"Who else was here?"
"Mr. Booth was here a long time lookin' everything over."
"How long ago?"

He scratched his beard and looked puzzled.

"Maybe an hour or so ago."

So that's where he had been while I was looking all over for him. Plotting his treasonous murder.

"Did he say where he was going?"
"Can't say for sure."

He shrugged his shoulders.

"Maybe to his room at the National."

I thanked him again and left the theater through the front door. A gusty wet night had blown in and I pulled the collar of my coat up to keep my face out of the wind. The gaslights made halos in the mist up and down the street. A street clock silently marked the rapidly passing time. 7:30.

It was a pretty good haul to the National, so it was after 7:45 when I arrived. The lobby was packed with people celebrating and having a good time. When I asked about Booth, the hotel clerk told me he had just left a few minutes ago. Bad news. Good news! Booth told the clerk he was headed to Herndon House. More bad news. Herndon House was back where I had just come from.

I thought I would take one last chance and try and find the

assassin before I had to go to the theater. When I arrived at Herndon House I finally had some good luck. The landlady said Booth was upstairs visiting a friend. It was now or never. I carefully crept up the stairs and looked for the room where I was told I could find Booth. The door was slightly open. My heart was pounding. I peeked in and cracked the door open just a little to see better. Suddenly I heard voices and footsteps coming down the hall. I darted into the room and scampered under the bed just as four men entered. I could tell from the tan riding boots one of them was Booth.

He spoke in low tones.

"Alright, Gentlemen, let's go over this one last time."

Through the lace of the bedspread I could dimly make out the men: one hulking giant, one short, bearded man and another person who didn't look much older than a boy. They were a motley crew compared to the well-groomed Booth.

"The most important thing is that we strike simultaneously. We want them to think that Washington City is full of assassins. It will throw the government into chaos. I will go to Ford's at 9:00 and assess the situation. At 10:15 I will kill the hairy monkey along with Grant if possible."

No one said a word and a chill hung heavy in the air.

Booth continued.

"At the same time Atzerodt will kill Vice-President Johnson at Kirkwood House."

He pointed to the short man with the beard.

"Cap'n?"

Booth grunted.

"I didn't know nothing about no killing. I thought we was just kidnapping and holding for ransom."

Booth shook his head.

"It's much too late for that. I've already prepared a letter to the newspapers informing them of our plans. I included each of your names. There's no turning back."

More silence.

"Before 10:15 young Davey will escort Payne to Secretary Seward's house. Now Davey (he pointed to the boyish looking man) you must stay to help Payne with his escape. If you leave he will get hopelessly lost. Is that understood?"

"Yes Captain, but Payne and me come up with an idea. We figured it would be easier to get into Seward's house if Payne pretended he had a prescription from the doctor with Seward being sick and all."

Booth slowly nodded.

"Good thinking, Herold. I suppose that might just work. Are you up to the task, Payne."

He gestured toward the hulking figure in the shadows.

"Yes, sir." Payne saluted.

"We will all meet at the Navy Yard Bridge and proceed to Surrattsville to pick up the rest of our weapons. If you get to the bridge and no one is there, go directly to Surrattsville. Is that understood?"

My mind was spinning so fast I couldn't even think straight. Booth was even more evil than I remembered. Not only did he plan to kill the President and General Grant, he had recruited this group of dimwits to help him spread murder and confusion all around Washington City. Was Secretary Seward the same William Seward that Harriet had told me about? This news of conspiracy really threw me for a loop. There was no earthly way I could stop all of them.

As the minutes passed, I couldn't help but notice how dusty it was under this bed where I was hiding. Whoever the maid was at Herndon House, she wasn't doing such a hot job. The dust bunnies were everywhere. There was one right in front of my nose. Then disaster struck. I felt the tickle first in my throat and then in the back of my nose. I tried to hold it in, but that sneeze was not going to be denied. "A-a-a-choo!"

They dragged me out from under the bed in about three seconds.

"YOU ARE NOT GOING TO GET AWAY WITH IT!"

Booth's eyes were blazing and he looked like he was going to go crazy.

"What in the devil!?... You again?... Hold him steady, Payne!"

The big ogre grabbed me and held me up by the waist. I

started to scream, but he clamped his dirty sweaty paw across my mouth. I tried to bite and kick him, but it didn't seem to bother him at all. I stopped struggling when I saw Booth pull out his knife. Just about that time my hat came off and my hair came tumbling down.

Booth sneered.

"Well, well, well. What do we have here? Those yellow stinking Yankees have to employ little girls for their spying now?"

He got up in my face and showed me his long silver knife.

"I think we all know what happens to spies, don't we? Hold her still Payne while I run her through."

I thought I was going to pass out.

Atzerodt jumped between us.

"Hold on now just a second, Cap'n. I didn't sign up for murder, and I sure didn't sign up for killin' no little girls. No tellin' who's goin' to hear us or find her or somethin' else terrible happenin'. Let's just get on with our business."

Booth lowered his knife and seemed to calm down a little. He ran his hand through his jet black hair.

"All right, but we can't just let her go."

He looked around.

"Payne, you have the key to this closet, do you not?"

Payne nodded and set me down. I knew enough to keep my mouth shut. Payne dug the key out of his pocket. They tied a filthy bandana around my mouth and tied my hands with some rope. Booth shoved me roughly into the empty closet and before he shut the door, he smiled at me and whispered in my ear.

"Our country owes all our troubles to Lincoln. God has simply made me the instrument of his punishment. When I leave that stage tonight, I will be the most famous man in America."

He threw my cap at me and laughed. The door shut. The key turned. I was in total darkness and there was a conspiracy of murderers riding wild through the streets of Washington City.

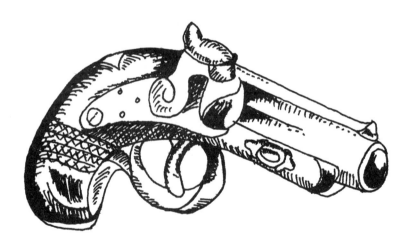

Chapter 12

Tesseract

April 14th, 1865, 8:37p.m. It had been such a long time since my dad woke me from my dream of dancing in the ballet. The rats, the soldiers, the dogs, the fear, the hunger, the wet, the cold. I hadn't let anything stop me. Until now. I had come so far and come so close to stopping Booth and preventing the murder of the man who had freed the slaves. The man who had kept the country from splitting in two. I felt like crying as I sat there in that dark, lonely closet.

8:42. If only I had told someone in Washington City about Booth. Maybe I wouldn't be sitting here with my mouth gagged by a disgusting cloth and my hands tied behind my back. It really made me angry when I thought about how Booth had bragged and laughed about killing the President. I kicked the floor. I gritted my teeth and screamed through the dirty rag. Only silence answered me.

8:45 In my anger I started grinding my teeth back and forth. To my surprise the cloth seemed to be getting looser. Maybe if I could chew through this smelly bandana, I could breathe a little easier. I had nothing to lose. I wasn't going anywhere soon. Thanks to all those years of chewing bubble gum, I had a strong set of choppers. I kept grinding and chewing, chewing and grinding. I tried not to think of what was causing that horrible taste in my mouth.

8:57 Success! I finally gnawed that rag in two, and shook

and spit free the remaining pieces. I started screaming and stomping my feet. If there was anyone left in Herndon House they were going to hear me.

9:13 I finally stopped yelling when I realized I was losing my voice. I tried to twist and turn the rope holding my hands, but Payne had tied me pretty tight. There wasn't much wiggle room, but I kept trying anyway. Since no one was answering my ruckus, getting my hands free was the only chance I had.

9:19 The rope was holding fast. The closet was very small, so it finally occurred to me that if I braced my feet forward and arched my back I could stand up. Once I got up I slammed my body repeatedly against the door and started yelling again. I jumped up and down like a maniac. No luck. The door wouldn't budge.

9:22 While I was flailing around like a fish out of water, my arm struck something on the back wall of the closet. I tried to reach it with my hands, but I could only feel it if I stood on my tiptoes. Someone had left a nail head sticking out of the wall about an inch. I was lucky I hadn't stabbed myself while I was jumping around. It felt rusty and sharp. Sharp? Sharp! I stood up as high as I could and started rubbing the rope against the head of the nail.

9:29 This was hard work. I was getting tired standing on my tiptoes, and I couldn't tell if I was making any progress.

9:38. I was about to give up when I felt the rope loosen just a tiny little bit. I worked even more feverishly and finally the rope gave enough for me to pull one hand and then another free. I had done it! I pounded on the door and yelled some more.

9:40 It was obvious that either there was no one else in Herndon House or all the people who lived there were deaf. They were probably out celebrating the end of the war. I was going to have to get out of here myself. I quickly took inventory. The only things I had in my pockets were a dime and a theater ticket. I started jerking and twisting the doorknob, but it seemed pretty sturdy. I knelt down and peered through the keyhole. All I could make out was the dim silhouette of the bed. As I stood back up the whistle Noodles had given me clanked against the doorknob. That was it! I frantically pulled the string off my neck and carefully pushed the whistle into the keyhole. I tried to turn it, but my hands were sweaty from all my jumping and banging. The whistle slid silenty into the keyhole and disappeared into the darkness. Darn! I hopefully and carefully turned the knob. Nothing. I sank to my knees in dispair.

9:43 While on the ground I noticed there were several good sized round holes in the floor. I got down on my face and stared into the biggest hole. Nothing but blackness. Was that someone's room down there? I shouted down into the hole. I got out my last dime and dropped it into the hole. It fit almost perfectly. If someone was sleeping down there maybe it would hit them and wake them up. I waited a few seconds and listened to hear it hit. Silence.

9:47 I didn't know what time it was, but I knew I had been in the closet for awhile. I wondered if the murder had already taken place. I felt sick to my stomach.

9:59 This closet had turned into a prison. A very small prison. Too bad it wasn't big enough for a family of four like my mom's and stepmonster's closets. At least then I could have a running start to try and knock the door down. I guess people then didn't need 45 pairs of shoes. Then it hit me.

There was one thing I hadn't tried. I turned my body to the short part of the closet. I put my feet against one wall and braced my back against the other. Using my hands to push me I realized that slowly but surely I could climb inch by inch up the wall. I found my hat, put it on and started going up.

10:03 I ran into one of those nails, it tore my coat and I lost my footing and had to start over again. I knew I could do it if I didn't move too quickly. I took off my coat, so I could feel the wall better. I moved my hands and then my feet about an inch at a time. More hard work. After what seemed like forever my head bumped into the ceiling. I carefully took one hand off the wall and started feeling around the ceiling. Just as my feet were slipping, my hand pushed open an attic door. I grabbed onto the open ledge and let my body fall. That almost jerked me loose, but somehow I pulled myself up. I was free.

10:04 I still couldn't see much, but I felt around the attic for some kind of door or handle that would set me free. I fumbled and stumbled frantically in the dark. As my eyes adjusted to the new space, I noticed a light from a window at the other side of the attic. I scrambled to the window and pushed it open. I leaped onto the sloping roof. It had stopped raining, but it was still slick and I lost my footing. I slid to the end, tried to catch myself and finally dropped with a thud onto the muddy ground. Ouch! I stuggled to my feet and noticed the clock across the street screaming out the time. Unbelievable.

10:06 I STILL HAD TIME TO STOP BOOTH. I couldn't prevent the other murders, but I still had a chance to save the President and General Grant. I was only a block and a half from Ford's. I hardly noticed that Washington City was lit up like a Christmas tree. I hardly noticed the row of gleaming, black carriages lined up along 10th Street in front of Ford's. I ran like a bear was chasing me. I ran like there were lives depending on me.

10:08 Sprinting up the steps, breathless into the lobby of Ford's theater, where is he, head swiveling, eyes searching, searching, no sign of the dastard, looking for the steps to the Dress Circle, hey wait a minute missy, you can't go in there, the play's going on, here's my ticket, ripping it from my pocket, slamming it on the counter, up, up more steps two at a time, where oh where is Booth, footlights, packed house, should I scream, the white door, no guard, where's the guard! my heart is pounding in my throat so hard I can't hear the people laughing at the play.

10:09 Calm down, breathe deep. Tick, tick, tick. No one is watching. Edge around to the white door. You're a soldier. You still have your cap. Act confident. No one will notice you. Everyone is watching the play. Slowly, carefully open the door. Slip in quietly. Close the door behind you.

I had done it! I slowly let the air out of my lungs. I just had to warn Lincoln. Which way? Then the hound of history caught up with me. The freezing hands surrounding my neck felt like death itself. There was Booth once again in my face. He must have been hiding behind the door. His eyes were liquid fire, his hands gripped me tighter.

"YOU AGAIN!" He hissed like a snake and I breathed in the poison of his alcohol. "I should have killed you when I had the chance. You SHALL NOT stop me!"

He was choking me so hard I could not breathe. He held me out by the neck with one hand, and in the blackness I could see him prop a board up against the door. No one was getting in. I struggled a little until I saw the knife gleaming in his pocket. I was losing consciousness. He put his free hand over my mouth and dragged me over by the door to the President's Box. Through my daze and the darkness I saw him look through a tiny hole that he must have made earlier in the day.

There I was. The hurricane of history howled around me. The dark murderous clouds swirled, but I was motionless in the calm eye, the very still point of destruction. Time slowed down, like a melting clock, drops of mercury falling one by one on a naked plate.

Booth loosened his grip.
I fell to my knees and clutched my throat.
He pulled out his terrible derringer.
Booth opened the door to the box.
I grabbed his leg and he kicked my bad eye with his riding boot.
I held on and he dragged me into the box.
Booth raised his gun to Lincoln's head.
I let out a silent scream.
The sound of the shot echoed through the theater.
Lincoln's head slumped forward.
Mrs. Lincoln screamed.
Blue smoke curled heavy in the air and filled the box.
Another man in the theater box jumped up and stuggled with Booth.
Booth sliced this man's arm to the bone with his knife.
Booth shouted, "Sic semper tyrannus" (thus it is to all tyrants) and moved to the edge of the box.
Just as he leaped toward the stage I grabbed the tail of his coat. He lost his balance and the spur of his right boot caught in the decorative flag hanging off the box.

I heard his ankle snap as he hit the stage.
Booth flashed his knife and limped off out of sight.

The scene in the box was one of complete destruction.
Lincoln's whiskered chin rested on his chest. Mrs. Lincoln's
face was white from shock. The stabbed man was rushing to
the outer door calling for a doctor. I had failed miserably. I
slumped to the floor in agony and exhaustion.

In my misery and through my one good eye I noticed my
soldier's cap on the ground. The cap that Minty had given me
looked lonely and forelorn on the floor of the smoky
President's Box. The only thing I had thought of the past five
days was saving President Lincoln. The thought of going
home or how I was going to get home had never once crossed
my mind. Through the haze I looked closely at the cap. I had
never really looked at it before. Right above the brass buckle
that overlapped the bill was an insignia. Two golden sabres
crossed right in the middle of the cap. And in the middle of
those two swords hung a black bead full of liquid, flecked
with silver and gold bubbles. I wearily pulled off the bead. I
took one last sorrowful look at President Lincoln, put the bead
in my mouth and swallowed hard.

I awoke in a groggy daze. The first person I saw was my
dad sitting there with a dumb look on his face. The only other
person in the room was a nurse dressed in white. It took me
about five minutes to realize I was in the first-aid station at
Tropicana Field. There was an ice bag on my swollen eye.
My dad smiled and hugged me really tight. I pulled him close
and started sobbing uncontrollably. The tension and emotion
of my rotten week just came flooding out.

"Oh, Daddy, Daddy, Daddy! I did the best I could. I tried

to save him, but I just couldn't do it! I just couldn't stop..."

I struggled to find the words, but they wouldn't come. I cried for a few minutes and Dad just held me and stroked my hair.

He whispered,

"It's o.k., Sweetheart. I know you did your best."

I pushed him away and stared deeply into his eyes.

"Then you know what happened?"
"Of course I do, Maggie. You're going to have a shiner for a few days, but you're going to be all right. Next time we have to remember to bring our gloves. Hey, look. Carl Crawford autographed the baseball that knocked you out!"

I knew it wouldn't do any good to try to explain, and I didn't feel like talking anyway. Dad put his arm around me and we slowly walked out into the cool night air. After we finally got in our car Dad said I could listen to any music I wanted to, but I said I didn't care. We listened to Ray Charles singing, "Take These Chains from my Heart." I tried not to think about all that had happened, but it kept running over and over again in my mind. I knew I was going to have to look in the library to see what happened to Booth and his band of murderers. I also wanted to find out more about Harriet and all the people and places she told me about.

I finally started to drift off to sleep and then I awoke with a start. I rubbed my tired eyes and squinted at my dad for a long, long time. It couldn't be true, could it? That day I saw those soldiers playing baseball on my way to

Washington City, something caught my eye. Something strangely familiar. That Union soldier standing on second base looked exactly like my dad.

"Hey, Pops, did you know they played baseball in the Civil War?"

"Really? I did not know that."

He turned to me and grinned like a baboon eating Dippin' Dots®.

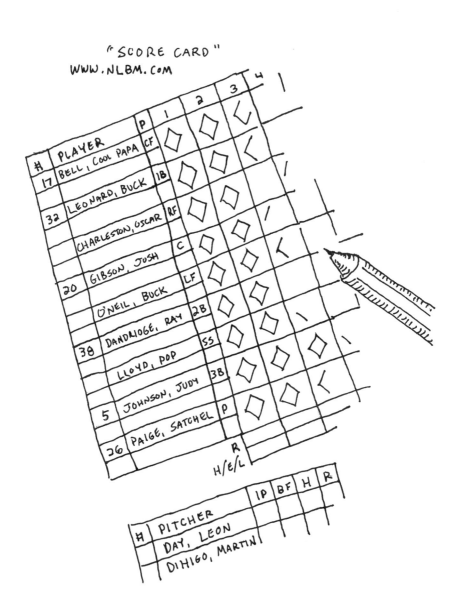

Maddie's Magic Markers was written, illustrated and published by its author, David Mark Lopez. Maddie's Magic Markers is intended to be a series of twelve historical adventures. If you have any comments or questions about the books, or have suggestions for Maddie's future travels please contact the author. He can be reached by phone at 239 947 2532, by mail at 3441 Twinberry Court, Bonita Springs, FL 34134 or by e-mail at www.davidmarklopez.com. He would love to know what you think of the books. If you would like to order additional copies of either book, simply fill out the form below and mail it along with your check or money order.

Name: _____

Address: _____

Phone #: _____

E-mail address: _____

Please send me _____ copies of
Walk Like an Egyptian @$6.00 per copy
(includes tax, postage and handling)

Please send me _____ copies of
Ride Like an Indian @$6.00 per copy
(includes tax, postage and handling)

Please send me _____ copies of
Run Like a Fugitive @$6.00 per copy
(includes tax, postage and handling)

Please send me _____ copies of
Fly Like a Witch @$6.00 per copy
(includes tax, postage and handling)

Mail to:
David Mark Lopez
3441 Twinberry Court
Bonita Springs, FL 34134